'I won't be kept in the castle like some bird in a cage.'

With an air of desperation tinging her voice, she said, 'You can't stop me from doing what I want.'

Sadiq looked down at the woman in front of him. The adrenalin was finally diminishing and being replaced by something hot and far more dangerous.

Giving in to the twisted inarticulate desires this woman roused inside him, he said throatily as he reached for her, 'I have no intention of stopping you doing anything once you're safe. But I *can* stop you driving me crazy.'

'What do you—?' Samia didn't get anything else out in time. Sadiq had pulled her into his tall, hard body with two hands and everything was blocked out when his head descended and his mouth unerringly found hers.

Abby Green got hooked on Mills & Boon® romances while still in her teens, when she stumbled across one belonging to her grandmother in the west of Ireland. After many years of reading them voraciously, she sat down one day and gave it a go herself. Happily, after a few failed attempts, Mills & Boon bought her first manuscript.

Abby works freelance in the film and TV industry, but thankfully the four a.m. starts and the stresses of dealing with recalcitrant actors are becoming more and more infrequent, leaving her more time to write!

She loves to hear from readers, and you can contact her through her website at www.abby-green.com She lives and works in Dublin.

Recent titles by the same author:

SECRETS OF THE OASIS
THE RESTLESS BILLIONAIRE*

Bad Blood

THE SULTAN'S CHOICE

BY
ABBY GREEN

First published in Great Britain 2011
by Mills & Boon, an imprint of Harlequin (UK) Limited,
Eton House, 18-24 Paradise Road, Richmond, Surrey TW9 1SR

© Abby Green 2011

ISBN: 978 0 263 22077 3

Harlequin (UK) policy is to use papers that are natural, renewable
and recyclable products and made from wood grown in sustainable
forests. The logging and manufacturing process conform to the
legal environmental regulations of the country of origin.

Printed and bound in Great Britain
by CPI Antony Rowe, Chippenham, Wiltshire

THE SULTAN'S CHOICE

This is for Ann K. Thank you for everything.

CHAPTER ONE

'I'm not marrying her for her looks, Adil. I'm marrying her for the myriad reasons she will make a good Queen of Al-Omar. If I'd wanted nothing but looks I could have married my last mistress. The last thing I need is the distraction of a beautiful woman.'

Princess Samia Binte Rashad al Abbas sat rigid with shock outside the Sultan of Al-Omar's private office in his London home. He hadn't been informed that she was there yet as he'd been on this call. His secretary, who had left momentarily, had inadvertently left his door slightly ajar—subjecting Samia to the deep rumble of the Sultan's voice and his even more cataclysmic words.

The drawling voice came again, tinged with something deeply cynical. 'That she may well appear, but certain people have always speculated that when the time came to take my bride I'd choose conservatively, and I'd hate to let the bookies down.'

Samia's cheeks burned. She could well imagine what the voice on the other end of the phone had said, something to the effect of her being *boring*.

Even if she hadn't heard this explicit conversation Samia already knew what the Sultan of Al-Omar planned to discuss with her. He wanted her hand in marriage. She hadn't slept a wink and had come here today half hoping that it would all be a terrible mistake. To hear him lay out in such bald terms that he was clearly in favour of this plan was shocking. And not only that but he evidently considered it to be a done deal!

She'd only met him once before, about eight years previously, when she'd gone to one of his legendary annual birthday parties in B'harani, the capital of Al-Omar, with her brother. Kaden had taken her before she'd gone on to England to finish her studies, in a bid to try and help her overcome her chronic shyness. Samia had been at that awfully awkward age where her limbs had had a mind of their own, her hair had been a ball of frizz and she'd still been wearing the thick bifocals that had plagued her life since she was small.

After an excruciatingly embarrassing moment in which she'd knocked over a small antique table laden with drinks, and the crowd of glittering and beautiful people had turned to look at her, she'd fled for sanctuary, finding it in a dimly lit room which had turned out to be a library.

Samia ruthlessly clamped down on *that* even more disturbing memory just as the Sultan's voice rose to an audible level again.

'Adil, I appreciate that as my lawyer you want to ensure I'm making the right choice, but I can assure you that she ticks all the boxes—I'm not so shallow that I can't make a marriage like this work. The stability and reputation of my country comes first, and I need a wife who will enhance that.'

Mortification twisted Samia's insides. He was referring to the fact that she was a world apart from his usual women. She didn't need to overhear this conversation to know that. Samia didn't want to marry this man, and she certainly wasn't going to sit there and wait for humiliation to walk up and slap her in the face.

* * *

Sultan Sadiq Ibn Kamal Hussein put down the phone, every muscle tensed. Claustrophobia and an unwelcome sense of powerlessness drove him up out of his leather chair and to the window, where he looked out onto a busy square right in the exclusive heart of London.

Delaying the moment of inevitability a little longer, Sadiq swung back to his desk where a sheaf of photos was laid out. Princess Samia of Burquat. She was from a small independent emirate which lay on his northern borders, on the Persian Gulf. She had three younger half-sisters, and her older brother had become the ruling Emir on the death of their father some twelve years before.

Sadiq frowned minutely. He too had been crowned young, so he knew what the yoke of responsibility was like. How heavy it could be. Even so, he wasn't such a fool to consider that he and the Emir could be friends, just like that. But if the Princess agreed to this marriage—and why wouldn't she?—then they would be brothers—in-law.

He sighed. The photos showed indistinct images of an average sized and slim-looking woman. She'd lost the puppy fat he vaguely remembered from when he'd met her at one of his parties. None of the pictures had captured her fully. The best ones were from last summer, when she'd returned from a sailing trip with two friends. But even in the press photos she was sandwiched between two other much prettier, taller girls, and a baseball cap was all but hiding her from view.

The most important consideration here was that none of the photos came from the tabloids. Princess Samia was not part of the Royal Arabian party set. She was discreet, and had carved out a quiet, respectable career as an archivist in London's National Library after completing her degree. For that reason, and many others, she was perfect. He didn't want a wife who would bring with her a dubious past life, or any whiff of scandal. He'd courted enough press attention himself over who he was dating or not dating. And to that end he'd had Samia thoroughly investigated, making sure there were no skeletons lurking in any closet.

His marriage would not be like his parents'. It would not be driven by mad, jealous rage and resemble a battlefield. He would not sink the country into a vortex of chaos as his father had done, because he'd been too distracted by a wife who'd resented every moment of being married to a man she didn't want to be married to. His father had famously pursued his mother, and it was common knowledge that in his obsession to have the renowned beauty reputed to be in love with another he'd paid her family a phenomenal dowry for her. His mother's constant sadness had driven Sadiq far away for most of his life.

He needed a quiet, stable wife who would complement him, give him heirs, and let him concentrate on running his country. And, above all, a wife who wouldn't engage his emotions. And from what he'd seen of Princess Samia she would be absolutely perfect.

With a sense of fatalism in his bones he swept all the photos into a pile and put them under a folder. He had no choice but to go forward. His best friends—the ruling Sheikh and his brother from a small independent sheikhdom within his borders—had recently settled down, and if he remained single for much longer he would begin to look directionless and unstable.

He couldn't avoid his destiny. It was time to meet his future wife. He buzzed his secretary. 'Noor, you can send Princess Samia in.'

There was no immediate answer, and a dart of irritation went through Sadiq. He was used to being obeyed the instant he made a request. Stifling that irritation because he knew it stemmed from something much deeper—the prospect of the demise of his freedom—he strode towards his door. The Princess should be here by now, and he couldn't avoid the inevitable any longer.

CHAPTER TWO

SAMIA'S hand was on the doorknob when she heard movement behind her and a voice.

'You're leaving so soon?'

It was low and deep, with the merest hint of a seductive accent, and she cursed herself for not leaving a split second earlier. But she'd dithered, her innately good manners telling her that she couldn't just walk out on the Sultan. And now it was too late.

Her back was stiff with tension as she slowly turned around, steeling herself against the inevitable impact of seeing one of the most celebrated bachelors in the world up close. She worked among dusty books and artefacts! She couldn't be more removed from the kind of life he led. There was no way he would want to marry her once he'd met her.

Every coherent thought fled her mind, though, when her eyes came to rest on the man standing just feet away. He filled the doorway to his office with his tall, broad-shouldered physique. His complexion was as dark as any man from the desert, but he had the most unusual blue eyes, piercing and seemingly boring right through Samia. Dressed in a dark suit which hugged his frame, he was six feet four of lean muscle—beautiful enough to take anyone's breath away. This was a man in his virile prime, ruler of a country of unimaginable wealth. Samia felt slightly light-headed for a moment.

He stood back and gestured with a hand into his office. 'I'm sorry to have kept you waiting. Please, won't you come in?'

Samia had no choice but to make her feet move in that direction. Her heart beat crazily as she passed him in the wide doorway and an evocative and intensely masculine scent teased her nostrils. She made straight for a chair positioned by the huge desk and turned around to see the Sultan pull the door shut behind him, eyes unnervingly intent on her.

He strolled into the room and barely leashed energy vibrated from every molecule of the man. Sensual elegance became something much more earthy and sexual as he came closer to Samia, and a disturbing heat coiled low in her belly.

His visage was stern at first, but then a wickedly sexy smile tugged at his mouth, sending her pulse haywire. Her thoughts scrambled.

'Was it something I said?'

Samia looked at him blankly.

'You were about to leave?' he elaborated.

Samia coloured hotly. 'No…of course not.' *Liar.* She went even hotter. 'I'm sorry… I just…'

She hated to admit it but he intimidated her. She might live a quiet existence and dislike drawing attention to herself—it was a safe persona she'd adopted—but she wasn't a complete shadow. Yet here she seemed to be turning into one.

Sadiq dismissed her stumbling words with one hand. He took pity on her obvious discomfort, but he was still reacting to the jolt running through him at hearing her voice. It was low and husky, and completely at odds with her rather mousy appearance. As mousy as the photos had predicted, he decided with a quick look up and down. In that trouser

suit and a buttoned up shirt which did nothing for her figure, it was imposible to make out if she *had* a figure.

And yet…Sadiq's keen male intuition warned him not to
make too hasty a judgement—just as a disconcerting tingle
of awareness skittered across his spine. He stuck his hands
into his pockets.

Samia could feel her cheeks heat up, and had a compel-
ling desire to look down and see where his trousers would be
pulled tight across his crotch. But she resolutely kept looking upwards. She tried to do the exercise she'd been taught
to deal with her blushing—which was to consciously *try* to
blush, and in doing so negate the reflexive action. But it was
futile. The dreaded heat rose anyway, and worse than usual.

He just looked at her. Samia valiantly ignored the heat
suffusing her face, knowing well that she'd be bright pink by
now, and hitched up her chin. She nearly died a small death
when he broke the tension and put out a hand.

'We've met before, haven't we?'

This was it—just what she'd been dreading. And it got
worse when he continued.

'I knew I remembered meeting you, but couldn't place
where it was. And then it came to me…'

Her heart stopped beating. She begged silently that it
wouldn't be that awful moment which was engraved on *her*
memory.

'You had an unfortunate tussle with a table full of drinks
at one of my parties.'

Samia was so ridiculously relieved that he didn't seem to
remember the library that she reached out to clasp his hand,
her own much smaller one becoming engulfed by long fingers. His touch was strong and warm and unsettling, and she
had to consciously stop herself from ripping her hand out of
his as if he'd stung her.

'Yes, I'm afraid that was me. I was a clumsy teenager.' Why did she sound breathless?

While still holding her hand, he was looking into her eyes and saying musingly, 'I didn't realise you had blue eyes too. Didn't you wear glasses before?'

'I had laser surgery a year ago.'

'Your colouring must come from your English mother?'

His voice was as darkly gorgeous as him. Samia nodded her head to try and shake some articulacy into her brain. 'She was half English, half Arabic. She died in childbirth with me. My stepmother brought me up.'

The Sultan nodded briefly and finally let Samia's hand go. 'She died five years ago?'

Samia nodded and tucked her hand behind her back. She found a chair behind her to cling on to. Her eyes darted away from that intense blue gaze as if he might see the bitterness that crept up whenever she was reminded of her stepmother. The woman had been a tyrant, because she'd always known she came a far distant second to the Emir's beloved first wife.

Samia looked back to the Sultan and her heart lurched. He was too good-looking. She felt drab and colourless next to him. How on earth could he possibly think for a second that she could be his queen? And then she remembered what he'd said about wanting a conservative wife and felt panicked again.

He indicated the chair she was all but clutching like a life raft. 'Please, won't you sit down? What would you like? Tea or coffee?'

Samia quelled an uncharacteristic impulse to ask for something much stronger. Like whisky. 'Coffee. Please.'

Sadiq moved towards his own chair on the other side of the desk and thankfully just then his secretary appeared with a tray of refreshments. Once she'd left, he tried not to notice the way the Princess's hand shook as she poured milk into her coffee. The girl was a blushing, quivering wreck, but she looked at him with a hint of defiance that he found curiously stirring. It was an intriguing mix when he was used to the brash confidence of the women he usually met.

He almost felt sorry for her as she handled the dainty cup. Miraculously it survived the journey from saucer to her mouth. She was avoiding his pointed look, so his gaze roamed freely over her and he had to concede with another little jolt of sensation that she wasn't really that mousy at all. Her hair was strawberry-blond, with russet highlights glinting in the late-afternoon sun slanting in through the huge windows. It was tied back in a French plait which had come to rest over one shoulder. Unruly curls had escaped to frame her face, which was heart-shaped.

She looked about eighteen, even though he knew she was twenty-five. And she was pale enough to have precipitated his question about her colouring. He'd forgotten that interesting nugget about her heritage.

It surprised him how clearly that memory of her knocking over the table had come back to him. He'd felt sorry for her at the time; she'd been mortified, standing there with her face beetroot red, throat working convulsively. Another memory hovered tantalisingly on the edges of his mind but he couldn't pin it down.

Absurdly long lashes hid her eyes. He had to admit with a flicker of *something* that she wasn't what he'd expected at all. Obeying some rogue urge to force her to look at him, so that he could inspect those aquamarine depths more closely, he drawled, 'So, Princess Samia, are you going to tell me why you were about to leave?'

Samia's eyes snapped up to clash with the Sultan's steady gaze. She couldn't get any hotter, and had to restrain herself from opening the top button of her shirt to feel some cool air on her skin. He was looking at her as if she were a specimen on a laboratory table. It couldn't be more obvious that she left him entirely cold, and that thought sent a dart of emotion through her.

'Sultan—' she began, and stopped when he put up a hand.

'It's Sadiq. I insist.'

The steely set of his face sent a quiver through her. 'Very well. Sadiq.' She took a deep breath. 'The truth is that I don't want to marry you.'

She saw the way his jaw tensed and his eyes flashed. 'I think it's usually customary to be asked for your hand in marriage before you refuse it.'

Samia's hands clenched tight on her lap. 'And I think it's customary to ask for the person's hand in marriage before assuming it's given.'

His eyes flashed dangerously and he settled back in the chair. Conversely it made Samia feel more threatened.

'I take it that you overheard some of my phone conversation?'

Samia blushed again, and gave up any hope of controlling it. 'I couldn't help it,' she muttered. 'The door was partially open.'

Sadiq sat forward and said brusquely, 'Well, I apologise. It wasn't meant for your ears.'

Giving in to inner panic, Samia stood up abruptly and moved behind the chair. 'Why not? After all, you were discussing the merits of this match, so why not discuss them here and now with me? Let's establish if I am conservative enough for you, or plain enough.'

A dull flush of colour across the Sultan's cheeks was the only sign that she'd got to him when she said that. Otherwise he looked unmoved by her display of agitation, and Samia cursed herself. Her hands balled on the back of the chair. He just sat back and regarded her from under heavy lids.

'You can be under no illusion, whether you heard that

conversation or not, that any marriage between us will be based purely on practicality along with a whole host of other considerations.'

When she spoke, the bitterness in Samia's voice surprised her. 'Oh, don't worry. I've no illusions at all.'

'This union will benefit both our countries.'

Suddenly a speculative gleam lit his eyes and he sat forward, elbows on the desk. Samia wanted to back away.

'I'd find it hard to believe that someone from our part of the world and culture of arranged marriages could possibly be holding out for a *love* match?'

He said this sneeringly, as if such a thing was pure folly. Feeling sick, Samia just shook her head. 'No. Of course not.' A love match was the last thing she would ever have expected or wanted. She had seen how love had devastated her father after losing her mother. She'd had to endure the silent grief in his gaze every time he'd looked at her, because *she'd* been the cause of her mother's death.

She'd seen how the ripples of that had affected everything—making his next wife bitter. Love had even wreaked its havoc on her beloved brother too, turning him hard as a rock and deeply cynical. She'd vowed long ago never to allow such a potentially destructive force anywhere near her.

The Sultan sat back again, seemingly pleased with her answer. He spread his hands wide. 'Well, then, what can you possibly have against this marriage?'

Everything! Exposure! Ridicule! Samia's hands were tightly clasped in front of her. 'I just…never saw it in my future.' She'd thought she'd faded enough into the background to avoid this kind of attention.

And then, as if he'd taken the words out of her brother's own mouth, Sultan Sadiq said with a frown, 'But as the eldest sister of the Emir of Burquat, how on earth did you think you would avoid a strategic match? You've done well to survive this far without being married off.'

Purely feminist chagrin at his unashamedly masculine statement was diminished when guilt lanced Samia. Her brother could have suggested any number of suitors before now, but hadn't. She'd always been aware that Kaden might one day ask her to make a strategic match, though, and this one had obviously been irresistible. This one came with economic ties that would help catapult Burquat into the twenty-first century and bring with it badly needed economic stability and development.

As much as she hated to admit it, they *did* come from a part of the world that had a much more pragmatic approach to marriage than the west. It was rare and unusual for a ruler to marry for something as frivolous as love. Marriages had to be made on the bedrock of familial ties, strategic alliances and political logic. Especially royal marriages.

If anything, this practical approach which eschewed love should appeal to her. She wasn't in any danger of falling for someone like Sadiq, and he certainly wouldn't be falling for her. She was almost certainly guaranteed a different kind of marriage from the one she'd witnessed growing up. Their children wouldn't be bullied and belittled out of jealous spite.

Sultan Sadiq stood up, and panic gripped Samia again. She moved back skittishly and cursed this mouse of a person she'd become in his presence. She ruled over thirty employees at the library, and was used to standing up to her brother, who was a man cut from the same dominant cloth as the Sultan, but mere minutes in *this* man's presence and she was jelly.

He prowled around the room, as if he couldn't sit still for longer than a second, and Samia recalled that he had a well known and insatiable love of extreme sports. He'd been the youngest ever sailor to take part in the prestigious Vendée

Globe race. As a keen sailor herself, she was in awe of that achievement.

In the tradition of men of his lineage he'd studied in both the UK and the US, and had trained at the exclusive royal military academy at Sandhurst. He had a fleet of helicopters and planes that he regularly flew himself. All in all he was a formidable man. Along with that came the notorious reputation of being one of the world's most ruthless playboys, picking up and discarding the most beautiful women in the world like accessories.

And every year—not that she needed to be reminded—he hosted the biggest, most lavish birthday party and raised an obscene amount of money for charity. For years after that humiliating incident at his party, she'd been scornful of the excess he presided over. But she'd seen the evidence of how much bona fide charity work he did when time after time he was lauded for his fundraising. And how did she know all this? Hours spent researching him on the internet last night, much to her shame.

He stopped pacing and quirked an ebony brow. 'Are you going to insist on refusing my offer of marriage and force me to look elsewhere for a wife?'

Samia heard the unimstakable incredulity in his voice. Patently he hadn't expected this to be hard. It gave her some much needed confidence back to see this chink in his arrogant armour.

'What would happen if I said no?'

He put his hands on narrow hips, and Samia's gaze couldn't help but drop for a moment to where his shirt was stretched across taut abdominal muscles. She could see the dark shadowing of a line of hair through the silk and her mouth dried. The physiciality of her reaction to him stunned her. No man had had this kind of effect on her before. It was as if she'd been asleep all her life and was gradually coming

to her senses here and now, in this room. It was most disconcerting.

'What would *happen*,' he bit out, 'is that the agreement
between your brother and I would be in serious jeopardy. I
would have to look to your next sister and assess her suitability.'

Samia blanched and her gaze snapped back up to Sadiq's.
'But Sara is only twenty-two.' And she jumped at her own
shadow, but Samia didn't say that. Immediately all her protective older sister hackles rose. 'She's entirely unsuitable
for you.'

Sadiq's gaze was glacial now. 'Which would seem to be a
running trend in your family, according to you. Nevertheless,
she would be considered. I would also be under no obliga-
tion to go through with my offer to help the Emir mine your
vast oil fields. He would be forced to look for expertise from
abroad, and that would bring with it a whole host of political challenges that I don't think Burquat can afford at this
moment in time.'

Samia tried to ignore the vision he was painting and smile
cynically. But her mouth tingled betrayingly when his gaze
dropped there for an incendiary moment. She fought to re-
tain her focus. 'And you're saying that your part in this is
entirely altruistic? Please don't insult my intelligence, no one
does anything for nothing in return.'

He inclined his head again, a different kind of gleam in
his eyes now. 'Of course not. In return I get a very suitable
wife—you, or your sister, which is entirely up to you. A
valuable alliance with a neighbouring kingdom and a slice
of the oil profits which I will funnel into a trust fund for our
children.'

Our children. Samia ignored the curious swooping sensation in the pit of her belly when he said those words.

'Burquat needs an alliance with one of its Arabian

neighbours, Samia. You know that as well as I do. On the brink of revealing to the world the veritable gold mine it harbours, it's in an acutely vulnerable position. Marriage to me will ensure my support. We will be family. You and your brother will be assured of my protection. We're also poised to sign a historic peace treaty. Needless to say our marriage would provide an even stronger assurance of peace between us.'

Every word he spoke was a death knell to Samia, and every word had already been spoken by her brother. She couldn't tell if the Sultan was bluffing about her sister or not, and didn't really want to test him. She also didn't want to investigate the dart of hurt that she should be so easily interchangeable with her sister. She didn't want him to choose her and she didn't want him to choose anyone else. Pathetic.

She could feel her life as she knew it slipping out of her grasp, but an inner voice mocked her. What kind of a life did she have anyway? Burying herself away in the library and quashing her naturally gregarious spirit after years of bullying by her stepmother wasn't something she could justify any more. Her stepmother was gone.

Even so, the prospect of moving out of that safe environment was still terrifying. Desperation tinged her voice. 'What makes you believe that I'll be a good wife? The right wife for you?'

The Sultan rocked back on his heels and put his hands in the pockets of his trousers. He was so tall and dark and forbidding in that moment.

'You are intelligent and have not lived your life in the public eye, like most of your peers. I think you are serious, and that you care about things. I read the article you wrote in the *Archivist* last month and it was brilliant.'

Samia felt humiliated more than pleased at his obvious research. An article in the *Archivist* only cemented how deeply *boring* she was. She did not need to be reminded of the disparity between her and the man in front of her. He was a playboy! The thought of the exposure she would face within a marriage to him made her feel nauseous. Because with exposure came humiliation.

Sadiq went on as remorselessly as the tide washing in. 'But apart from all of that you are a princess from one of the oldest established royal families in Arabia and you were born to be a queen. God forbid, but if something happened to your brother tomorrow you would be next in line for your throne. If we were married then you would not have to shoulder that burden alone, and I would make sure that Burquat retained its emirate status.'

Samia felt herself pale. She knew she was next in line to the throne of Burquat, but had never really contemplated the reality of what that meant. Kaden seemed so invincible that she'd never had to. But Sultan Sadiq was right; she was in a very delicate position. She might know the theory of ruling a country, but the reality was a different prospect altogether. And she knew that not many other potential husbands would guarantee that Burquat retained its autonomy. Al-Omar was huge and thriving, and the fact that the Sultan saw no need to bolster his own power through annexing a smaller country made Samia feel vulnerable—she hadn't expected this.

Afraid that he would see something of the turmoil she felt, she turned to face a window which looked out over manicured lawns—a serene and typically English tableau which would normally be soothing.

She felt short of breath and seriously overwhelmed. There was a point that came in everyone's life when a person was called to make the starkest of choices, and she was facing hers right now. Not that she really had a choice. That was becoming clearer and clearer.

But, desperate to cling on to some tiny measure of illusion,

Samia turned around again and bit her lip before saying to the Sultan, 'This is a lot to take in. Yesterday I was facing only the prospect of returning to Burquat to help oversee the refurbishment of our national library, and now...I'm being asked to become Queen of Al-Omar.' She met his blue gaze. 'I don't even know you.'

A flash of irritation crossed the Sultan's face, shadowing those amazing eyes, and inwardly Samia flinched at this evidence of his dispassionate and clinical approach to something so momentous.

'We have our lifetimes to get to know one another. What won't wait, however, is the fact that I need to marry and have heirs. I have no doubt in my mind, Princess Samia, that you are the one who was born to take that position.'

Samia tried not to look as affected by his words as she felt. He was only saying it like that because he'd decided she'd make him a good wife and wasn't prepared to take no for an answer. At another time she might almost have smiled. He reminded her so much of her autocratic brother.

She knew for a fact that there were many women who would gladly trample over her to hear him speak those words to them. And she wished right now that one of them was standing there instead of her—even though her belly did a curious little flip when she thought of it.

'I just...' She stopped ineffectually. 'I need some time to think about this.'

Sadiq's face tightened ominously, and Samia had the feeling that she'd pushed him too far. With that came a sense of panic that...what? He'd choose her sister instead? That he'd send her away and tell her to have a nice life? And why was that making her feel panicky when it was exactly what she wanted?

But an urbane mask closed off any expression on that hard-jawed face, and after an interminable moment he said softly, 'Very well. I will give you twenty-four hours. This time tomorrow evening I expect you to be back here in this room to tell me what you have decided.'

Sadiq stood at the window of his private sitting room, three floors above the office where he'd just met Princess Samia. He looked out over the city of London bathed in dusky light. The scent of late-summer blossoms was heavy in the air. He suddenly missed the intense heat of his home—the sense of peace that he got only when he knew that the vast expanse of Al-Omari desert was within walking distance.

Irritation snaked through him at the realisation that due to Samia's patent reluctance he'd be forced to spend longer in Europe than he wanted to. He could see his discreet security men in front of his house—necessary trappings for a head of state—but he was oblivious to all that. For once he wasn't consumed with thoughts of politics, or the economy, or women.

He frowned. Well, that wasn't entirely true. One woman *was* consuming his thoughts, and for the first time in his life it wasn't accompanied with the enticing sense of expectation at the prospect of bedding her. And then he had to concede that it had been a long time since pure expectation had precipitated *any* liaison with a lover—it was more likely to be expectation mixed with a lot of cynicism.

Sadiq's frown became deeper, grooving lines into his smooth forehead. Since when had he acknowledged the fact that for him bedding women was accompanied by a feeling of ennui and ever deepening cynicism? He suspected uncomfortably that it was long before he'd witnessed his close friends' weddings in Merkazad.

Seeing his friends wearing their hearts on their sleeves had induced a feeling of panic and had pushed a button—a button that had been deeply buried and packed under years of cynical block building and ice. Perhaps that was what had precipitated his decision to marry? This impulse to protect himself at all costs—a desire to negate what he'd seen at Nadim and Salman's weddings. The need to prove that he wasn't ever going to succumb to that awful uncontrollable emotion again.

Even now he could remember that day, and the excoriating humiliation of baring his heart and soul to a woman who had all but laughed in his face.

In choosing to marry someone like Princess Samia he would be safe for ever from such mortifying episodes, because he was in no danger of falling in love with her. He was also safe from falling in lust. She was too pale, too shapeless. His stomach clenched... Funnily enough, though, he couldn't get those enigmatic aquamarine eyes out of his head. And he had to concede she wasn't *un*pretty. But she certainly wasn't beautiful. He'd always accepted that the wife he picked would fulfil a role—an important one. As such, to find her attractive would be a bonus and a luxury. His responsibility to his country was greater than such frivolous concerns.

Altogether, she wasn't as unappealing as he might have feared initially. He grimaced. He'd had his fair share of the world's beauties. It was time to convert his lust into building up a country unrivalled in its wealth and economic stability. He needed focus for that, and a wife like Samia would provide that focus. He wouldn't be distracted by her charms, and clearly she was not the coquettish type, so she wouldn't waste time trying to charm him.

Sadiq's frown finally cleared from his face and he turned his attention to the rolling business news channel on the muted television screen in the background. Despite the Princess's reluctance he had no doubt that she would return the next day and give him the answer he expected. The alternative was simply inconceivable.

CHAPTER THREE

24 hours later

'I'M not going to marry you.'

Sadiq's mouth was open and he was already smiling urbanely in anticipation of the Princess's acquiescence— already thinking ahead to buying her a trousseau and getting her out of those unflattering suits. Her bottom had barely touched the seat of the chair opposite him. He frowned. Surely she couldn't have just said—

'I said I don't want to marry you.'

Her voice was low and husky, but firm, and it tugged somewhere deep inside him again. Sadiq's mouth closed. She sat before him like a prim nun, hair pulled back and dressed in a similarly boxy suit to the one she'd worn yesterday. This one was just a slightly darker hue of blue. Not a scrap of make-up enhanced those pale features or those aquamarine eyes. Disconcertingly, at that moment he noticed a splash of freckles across her delicately patrician nose.

Freckles. Since when had he noticed freckles on anyone? Any woman of his acquaintance would view freckles with the same distaste as acne. Something nebulous unfurled within Sadiq, and he sat back and realised that it was a surprise—because it was so long since anyone had said no to him. Or been so reluctant to impress him. Princess Samia's chin lifted minutely, and for a second Sadiq could see her innately regal hauteur. She might be the most unprepossessing princess he'd ever met, but she was still royalty and she couldn't hide it.

The thin line of her mouth drew his focus then, and bizarrely he found himself wondering how full and soft those lips would be when relaxed...or kissed. Would they be pink and pouting, begging for another kiss?

Samia could see the conflict on the Sultan's face, the clear disbelief. That was why she'd repeated herself. It had been as much to check she hadn't been dreaming. She was trembling all over like a leaf. She'd tossed and turned all night and had kept coming back to the stark realisation that she really did not have a choice.

But when faced with Sadiq again, and the clear expectation on his face that she was there to say yes, she had felt some rebellious part of her rise up. This was her only chance of escaping this union. She crushed the lancing feeling of guilt. She couldn't worry now about the fallout or she'd never go through with it. The thought of marrying this man was just so downright threatening that she had to do something— no matter how selfish it felt.

Sadiq's voice rumbled over her, causing her pulse to jump. 'There's a difference between *not* marrying me, and not *wanting* to marry me. One implies that there is no room for discussion, and the other implies that there is. So which is it, Samia?'

Samia tried to avoid that searing gaze. He was sitting forward, elbows on his desk, fingers steepled together. The way he said her name made her feel hot. She was already unravelling at the seams because she was facing this man again, even though the heavy oak desk separated them. Even the threat to her sister wasn't enough right now to make her reconsider. She'd cross that bridge if it came to it.

He hadn't kept her waiting today. He'd been waiting for her. Standing at his window like a tall, dark and gorgeous spectre. And now he was utterly indolent—as if they might be discussing the weather. He wore a shirt and no tie. The top button was undone, revealing the bronzed column of his throat. The sleeves of his shirt were rolled up, showing off muscled forearms more suited to an athlete than a head of state. Samia felt unbearably restless all of a sudden.

Abruptly she stood up, wanting to put space between them. She couldn't seem to sit still around this man, and she couldn't concentrate while he was looking at her like that—as if she were under a microscope. So clinically.

She went and stood behind the chair, breathing erratically. 'Discussion…' she finally got out. 'Defintely the discussion one.'

Great. Now she couldn't string a sentence together—and what was she doing, encouraging a discussion with one of the world's greatest debaters? She paced away from the chair, feeling constricted in her suit. She'd never been as self-conscious about what she wore as she had been in the last thirty-six hours. Samia had always been supremely aware of her own allure, or more accurately the lack of it, and was very comfortable with a uniform of plain clothes to help her fade into the background. Or at least she had been till now.

She avoided his eye. 'Look, I know you need a wife, and on paper I might look like the perfect candidate—'

Sadiq cut in with a low voice. 'You *are* the perfect candidate.' He stifled intense irritation. She was the *only* candidate. After carefully vetting potentially suitable brides from his world and dismissing them, she was the only one he'd kept coming back to. And once he'd set his mind on something he would not rest until he had full compliance. Failure was not an option.

Samia turned back to face him, and quailed slightly under

the glowering look he was sending her. 'But I'm not! You'll see.' She searched frantically for something to say. 'I don't go out!'

'A perfectly commendable quality. Despite what you've been led to believe, I'm not actually the most social of animals.'

Samia forced her mind away from that nugget of information. This man and a quiet evening in by the fire just did *not* compute. 'You find it commendable that I don't have a life? That's not something to applaud—it's something to avoid. How can I be your queen when the last party I was at was probably yours? You must have parties every week—you move in those circles. I wouldn't know what to do...or say.'

Samia's tirade faltered, because the Sultan had moved and was now sitting on the edge of the desk, one hip hitched up. She swallowed and wished he hadn't moved. Heat was rising, and dimly she wondered if he had any heating on.

'Of course you'd know what to do and say. You've been brought up to know *exactly* what to do and say. And if you're out of practice you'll learn again quickly enough.'

Samia choked back her furious denial. She ran a hand through her hair impatiently, which was something she did when she was agitated. She forgot that it was tied back and felt it come loose but had to ignore it.

She faced him fully. 'You really don't want me for your wife. I don't like parties. I get tongue-tied when I'm faced with more than three people, I'm not sophisticated and polished.' *Like all your other women.* Samia just about managed not to let those words slip out.

Sadiq was watching the woman in front of him with growing fascination. She *wasn't* sophisticated and polished—and he suddenly relished that fact for its sheer uniqueness. She was literally coming apart in front of him, revealing someone very different from the woman she was describing. He agreed with absolutely everything she was saying—apart from the bit about her not being a suitable wife.

'And yet,' he drawled, 'you've been educated most of your life in a royal court, and your whole existence has held within it the potential for this moment. How can you say you're not ready for this?'

Samia could feel the unfashionably heavy length of her hair starting to unravel down her back. Her inner thermostat was about to explode. With the utmost reluctance she opened her jacket, afraid that if she didn't she'd melt in a puddle or faint.

Before she could stop him Sadiq was reaching out and plucking the coat from her body as easily as if she were a child, placing it on the chair she'd vacated. Too stunned to be chagrined, Samia continued, 'You need someone who is used to sophisticated social gatherings. I've been in libraries for as long as I can remember.'

The ancient library in the royal Burquat castle had always been her refuge from the constant taunting of her stepmother, Alesha. She started to pace again, disturbed by Sadiq's innate cool.

'You need someone who can stand up to you.' She stopped and stood a few feet away, facing him. She *had* to make him see. 'I had a chronic stutter until I was twelve. I'm pathologically shy. I'm so shy that I went to cognitive behavioural therapy when I was a teenager to try and counteract it.' Which had precipitated another steady stream of taunts and insults from her stepmother, telling her that she would amount to nothing and never become a queen when she couldn't even manage to hold a conversation without blushing or stuttering.

Sadiq had stood up and come closer to Samia while she'd been talking. He was frowning down at her now, arms folded across that impressive chest. 'You don't have a stutter any more, and I'd wager that your therapist, if he or she was any good, said that you were just going through a phase that any teenager might go through. And plenty of children suffer from stuttering. It's usually related back to some minor incident in their childhood.'

Samia blinked. She felt as if he could see inside her head to one of her first memories, when she had been trying to get her new stepmother's attention and was stuttering in her anxiety to be heard. She would bet that *he'd* never gone through anything like that. But he'd repeated more or less exactly what her therapist had said. It was so unexpected to hear this from him of all people that any more words dried in her throat as he started to move around her.

Sadiq was growing more intrigued by the second. Her hair had come completely undone by now, and it lay in a wavy coil down her back. His fingers itched to reach out and loosen it. It looked silky and fragrant...a little wild. It was at such odds with that uptight exterior.

So close to her like this, for the first time he noticed the disparity in their heights. She was a lot smaller than the women he was used to, and he felt a surprising surge of something almost *protective* within him. With the jacket gone he could see that she was slight and delicate, yet he sensed a strength about her—an innate athleticism. He could see the whiteness of her bra strap through her shirt, and how her shirt was tucked into the trousers, drawing his eye to a slim waist and the gentle flare of her hips. He didn't think he'd ever seen a prospective lover so demurely dressed, and that thought caught him up short. She was to be his *wife*. Lovemaking would be purely functional. If he got any enjoyment out of it, it would be a bonus.

He came to stand in front of her and could see where she'd opened the top button of her shirt, revealing the slender length of her neck right down to the hollow at the base

of her throat. It looked pink and slightly dewed with mois-
ture. She must be hot. He had the most bizarre urge to push
her shirt aside and press a finger there. His eyes dropped
again, and he could see very plainly the twin thrusts of her
breasts, rising and falling with her breath and fuller than he
had first imagined.

To his utter shock, the unmistakable and familiar spark
of desire lit within him. With more difficulty than he would
have liked, he brought his gaze back up to hers and felt a
punch to his gut at the way those aquamarine depths suddenly looked as dark blue as the Arabian sea on a stormy
day. Tendrils of hair were curling softly around her face, and
she looked softer, infinitely more feminine. In fact in that
moment she looked almost...beautiful. Sadiq reeled at this
completely unexpected development.

Samia was helpless under Sadiq's assessing gaze. No man
had ever looked at her so explicitly, his gaze lingering on
her breasts like that. And yet she wasn't insulted or shocked.
A languorous heat was snaking through her veins. She was
caught in a bubble. A bubble of heat and sensation. As soon
as he had walked behind her she'd had to undo her top button because she couldn't breathe—she'd felt so constricted.
And now he was looking at her as though...as though—

'You say I need someone to stand up to me and that's what
you've been doing since yesterday.' His beautifully sculpted
mouth firmed. 'It's a long time since anyone has refused my
wishes. I encounter people every day who are overawed and
inhibited by what they perceive me to be and yet I don't get
that from you.' Before Samia could articulate anything, he
continued. 'Very few people would feel they had the author-
ity to do that, but we're the same, Princess Samia, you and I.'

Samia nearly blanched at that. If there was one thing she
was sure of, it was that she and this man were *not* the same.

Not in a million years. Polar opposites. 'We're not the same,' she got out painfully. 'Really, we're not.'

He ignored her. 'I know you've got a closely knit and loyal group of friends.'

Without a hint of self-pity and vaguely surprised that he knew this, she said, 'That says more about who I am and the background I come from than anything else.' Remembering one painful episode in college, she went on, 'I could never fully trust that people weren't making friends just because they thought they could get something out of me.' When he still looked unmoved she said desperately, 'I'm boring!'

He arched an incredulous brow. 'Someone who is boring doesn't embark on a three-woman trip across the Atlantic in a catamaran made out of recycled materials in a bid to raise awareness about the environment.'

Samia was immediately disconcerted. 'You know about that?'

He nodded and looked a little stern. 'I think it was either one of the most foolhardy or one of the bravest things I've ever seen.'

She flushed deeper and couldn't stop a dart of pleasure rushing through her at the thought she'd earned this man's admiration. 'I care about the environment... The other two were old friends from college, and they couldn't raise the funding required on their own... But once I got involved...' Her voice trailed off, her modesty not wanting to make it sound as if she'd been instrumental in the project.

Sadiq rocked back on his heels. 'I have a well-established environmental team in Al-Omar that could do with your support. I often find I'm too tied up with other concerns to give it my full attention. We've both grown up in rarefied environments, Samia, both grown up being aware of public duty. If anything, your teenage and childhood experiences will make you more empathetic with people—an essential quality in any queen.'

Samia objected to his constant avowal of partnership, and the tantalising carrot of being able to work constructively for the environment, but her attempt to halt him in his tracks with a weak-sounding 'Sadiq...' made no impact.

'You might find social situations intimidating, but with time they'll become second nature. Also, you can't deny that having grown up as a princess in a royal court you are aware of castle politics and protocol. You would have learnt that by osmosis. These are all invaluable assets to me in any marriage I undertake. I don't have the time or the inclincation to train someone.'

Samia blinked up at him again. She couldn't deny it. As much as she might want to. Even though she'd spent her formative years avoiding her stepmother, she knew castle politics like the back of her hand—she'd had to learn to survive. Her knowledge of the things he spoke had been engraved invisibly on her psyche like a tattoo from birth.

'I want to create a solid alliance between Al-Omar, Merkazad and Burquat. We live in unstable times and need to be able to depend on each other. Marrying you will ensure a strong alliance with your brother. I already have it with Merkazad. Your father's rule put Burquat firmly in an isolated position, which did your country no favours. Thankfully your brother is reversing that stance. I don't see how you have any grounds at all—apart from your own personal concerns—to believe that you are not fit to become my queen, and in so doing ensure the future stability of your country.'

Samia swallowed painfully, glued to his glittering blue eyes in sick fascination. He was right. She could no more stand there and deny these facts than she could deny her very heritage and lineage. She might have hidden herself away in a college and then a dusty library for the past few years, but she'd always had the knowledge of this ultimate responsibility within her.

And her concerns *were* personal—selfish, in fact. She just did not have that luxury. She wasn't the same as the average person on the street. She had obligations, responsibilities.

As if he could sense her weakening, Sadiq moved closer and Samia's breath faltered. That embarrassing heat was back, rising inexorably through her body, and for the first time she recognised it not as the heat of embarrassment or shyness but as a totally different kind of heat. The heat of desire. The fact that he was having the same inevitable effect on her as every other woman he must encounter was humiliating. She was not immune.

'I...' She had to swallow to get her voice to work. He was standing so close now that all she could see was those dark blue irises, sucking her in and down into a vortex of nebulous needs she'd never felt before. She battled her own sapping will and focused. 'I accept what you're saying. They're all valid points.'

'I know they are.'

Had his voice dropped an octave? It sounded like it. They were standing so close now that Samia could feel his warm breath feather around her, could smell the intensely masculine scent of sandalwood and musky spice. It was the memory of that scent that had kept her awake for long hours last night.

To her utter shock he reached out a hand and touched his thumb to her bottom lip, tugging it. She had the most bizarre urge to flick out her tongue and taste his finger. Her heart slowed to about a beat a minute.

'That's better. You shouldn't be so tense. You have a very pretty mouth.'

A pretty mouth? No one had ever referred to her as pretty

in her life. Instantly Samia felt as if a cold bucket of water had been flung over her. She stepped back abruptly, forcing the Sultan's hand down, breaking the spell. Clearly the man felt the need to placate her with false compliments. What was wrong with her? Believing for half a second that she was in some sensual bubble with the Sultan of Al-Omar who had courted and bedded some of the world's greatest beauties?

Her face flaming again, Samia looked away and tried to regain control, breathing a sigh of relief when she sensed Sadiq move back too.

His voice was tight. 'Samia, it's inevitable. You might as well give in now, because I won't. Not until you say yes.'

She gulped and shook her head. Words were strangled in her throat. She was more sure than ever that she couldn't do this. Especially after she'd all but sucked his finger into her mouth like some wanton groupie!

She heard him sigh expressively and sneaked a look. He was glancing at his watch and then looking at her. 'I don't know about you but I'm hungry. I've had a busy day.'

Samia just looked at him stupidly for a moment. The tension in the atmosphere diminished. And then her stomach gurgled loudly at the thought of food. She'd been so wound up for the last thirty-six hours that she'd barely eaten a thing.

As if Sadiq could see the turmoil on her face he quirked his mouth and came close again, playing havoc with Samia's hearbeat, and tipped up her chin with a finger.

'Rest assured I won't stop until you have agreed to become my wife and queen. But we might as well start to get to know one another a little better in the meantime. And eat.'

Before she knew what was happening Sadiq was leading the way from the study with her jacket over his arm. She opened her mouth to protest, but then they were in the hall and he was conferring with his butler who bowed and indicated for Samia to follow Sadiq into what turned out to be a dining room.

It was more than impressive. Dark walls were lined with portraits of Sadiq's ancestors in western dress, looking very exotic, a huge gleaming oak table dominated the room and there was a setting for two at the top of the table.

Sadiq was standing behind a chair, looking at her expectantly, and, feeling very weak, Samia went forward and sat down. There was a flurry of activity as the butler came back with more staff and they were presented with options for dinner. Samia made her choice without even thinking about what she was ordering.

When they were momentarily alone Samia bit her lip for a moment and began to speak, not even sure what she wanted to say. 'Sadiq...'

But he just poured her a glass of chilled white wine and said disarmingly, 'You made the right choice with the fish. Marcel, our chef, is an expert. He used to work for the Ritz in Paris.'

Samia took the proffered glass and felt her unruly hair slip over her shoulder. She'd long lamented the fact that her hair didn't fall in sleek and smooth waves like her younger sisters', who'd all inherited their own mother's exotic dark colouring. Kaden had inherited their father's dark looks, so she'd always been the odd one out. Her stepmother had only had to breathe air into Samia's own sense of isolation to compound it.

She felt a little naked with her hair down like this— somehow exposed, as if some secret feminine part of herself was being bared to the sun. It wasn't altogether uncomfortable, which made it even more disturbing. Sadiq sat back and smiled at Samia urbanely, making her stomach flip-flop. If he turned on the charm she didn't know how she would cope.

As if privy to her private thoughts, that was exactly what he did.

For the next hour and a half, while they ate delicious food, he managed to draw Samia out of her shell. At first she did her best to resist, but it was like trying to resist the force of a white water rapid. Something was happening—some intangible shift.

Perhaps she'd started feeling this softening, melting sensation when he'd mentioned her sailing trip? Or perhaps it had been his easy acceptance when she'd told him about her stuttering and shyness. She'd never told anyone about that before, and had done so with him purely in a bid to repel him. But it hadn't worked. He'd *empathised*. It was almost like a betrayal to witness the sudden ease with which she was finding herself talking to him now, albeit about superficial subjects.

He was disarming her enough to make her forget for a moment who he was. It was seductive evidence of a self-deprecating side, and of the undeniable bond they shared in both coming from the same part of the world, from a similar background. Everything he had already pointed out. She had not expected self-deprecation from this man, or any kind of feeling of kinship with him. She hadn't expected him to defuse the tension like this.

They were finishing their coffee when Samia looked at Sadiq, somewhat emboldened after the meal and a glass of wine. 'You're very good you know,' she said.

He quirked a brow, his eyes breathtakingly blue against the olive tone of his skin. 'Good? In what way?'

Samia had to concentrate. It was like sitting across the table from a Hollywood heart-throb, not a head of state. 'At charming people.'

He shrugged minutely, and for a second Samia saw something stern flash across his face and into those eyes.

Immediately the warm bubble of fuzziness that had been infusing her dissipated. Of *course*. How could she have been so silly? This was all an act—an act put on her for benefit and his, to get to her to acquiesce to his plans for marriage. Of course he was charming her. And she was falling for it and believing it like any other woman with a pulse would.

She made a point of looking at her watch, even though she didn't register the time, and then looked back at Sadiq, tensing herself against his effect on her.

'I have to be up early tomorrow. I'm still handing over to my successor.'

Sadiq sat forward. 'You like working in the library here?'

That rebellious streak rising again, Samia said defiantly, 'Yes. And a queen who is more at home surrounded by books is hardly the queen for *you*.'

Sadiq had to quell the sudden urge to wipe that prim look off Samia's face by kissing her. He'd had her in the palm of his hand during the meal—he knew it. She'd been more relaxed than he'd seen her. And with that had come the realisation that he had grossly underestimated her appeal. The spark of desire that had lit earlier had erupted into full-on lust as he'd watched her natural effervescence emerge.

She'd blossomed quite literally before his eyes—like a flower being exposed to heat and light after being hidden in a dark corner. It was the most amazing thing. She reminded him of a dimond in the rough. Actually, he amended, more like a dark and glowing yellow diamond. A rare jewel.

But now she'd clammed up again like an oyster shell, protecting the bounty within. Those full lips were once again a thin line, the eyes downcast. He signalled discreetly to his staff and rose smoothly to his feet once his wayward body felt more under control. A dart of satisfaction went through him at seeing Samia look confused for a moment, as if she'd expected him to challenge her. And then she rose to her feet too, somewhat less assuredly, and that protective instinct surged again. Sadiq had to clench his hands to fists to stop himself reaching out to steady her.

He couldn't understand his physical response. The last woman he'd been with had been hailed as the most beautiful woman in the world three years running. And there had never been one moment when he'd felt protective of *her*. When he tried to picture her now all he remembered was that his desire for her had waned long before he'd admitted it to himself. And yet *this* woman, whose appeal was more wholesomely pretty than beautiful, was having a more incendiary effect on his libido than he could remember.

As Samia preceded Sadiq out of the dining room, he thought of something to test her. She got to the front door and turned around. Clearly she was hoping he wouldn't challenge her again. He almost pitied her for her blind optimisim. He handed her her jacket and watched her expression closely.

'You know,' he mused, 'perhaps you're right after all. Perhaps you're *not* suitable to be my wife.'

Something suspiciously exultant moved through him as he caught the split second of a reaction she couldn't hide because her face was just too expressive.

Samia opened her mouth, but nothing came out. She stilled in the act of putting her jacket on. He'd completely surprised her. And, to her utter chagrin, instead of feeling relieved she had the absurd desire to contradict him and tell him that she *could* be a good wife for him. What was going on?

She tried desperately to hide her confusion as she continued putting on her jacket. 'You mean if I was to walk out of here right now you wouldn't stop me? Or pursue this matter?'

Sadiq smiled, but it was the smile of a shark. 'You don't really believe I'm just going to let you walk away, do you?'

Anger rose bright and rapid at the realisation that he was

playing with her. Samia grabbed for the door and tried to wrench it open, but it wouldn't budge. She turned back, exasperated at being trapped. 'If your door worked you could watch me walk out right now, and there wouldn't be one thing you could do about it.'

Samia was mortified, because she knew well that he'd caught her out. She'd shown her reaction before she could hide it. He *knew* how conflicted she was about this.

'The door works fine, Samia. I just wanted to see how you'd react if you got a sniff of freedom, and your face told me all I need to know.'

Acting on a purely animal instinct to escape a threat, Samia turned back to the door and this time it opened. She stood in the doorway, breathing deep, and almost simultaneously lights exploded all around her.

The paparazzi.

Samia heard a colourful Arabic curse behind her even as she registered big burly bodyguards materializing as if from thin air to hold the photographers back. Strong arms came around her and pulled her into a lean and hard muscled body. Samia was plastered against Sadiq's length as he all but carried her back over the threshold and into the house.

It took a second for her to register that it was quiet again and the door was shut behind them. Samia's breath sounded laboured, and she realised that she was still clamped to Sadiq like a limpet. Breasts crushed to his chest. She scrambled backwards, face flaming.

Sadiq raked a hand through his hair. 'Are you okay? I'm sorry about that. Sometimes they lie in wait once they know I'm here, and the bodyguards can't do anything.'

He could still feel the imprint of her body—the firm swells of her breasts pressed against him just for that brief moment. How delicate she'd been. She'd fit into his body like a missing jigsaw piece. For someone used to women who almost matched him in height, it had been a novel sensation.

She was standing there, looking dishevelled and innocently sexy with colour high in her cheeks, and he knew that she had no idea how alluring she was—which only inflamed him more, because he was used to women being all too aware of their so-called allure.

'You *knew* about that.'

He frowned, not liking the accusatory tone in her voice. 'What do you mean?'

'You just said that you know they lie in wait. I'm going to be all over the papers with you. Leaving your house.'

Samia realised she was shaking violently. She heard another curse and felt Sadiq take her arm in a firm grip. 'Come back into the study. You're in shock.'

Once in the big stately room, Sadiq all but pressed Samia down into a chair and went to get a tumbler of brandy. He came back and handed it to her. 'Take a sip. You'll feel better in a minute.'

Hating feeling so vulnerable, Samia took the glass and a gulp of the drink, coughing slightly. She watched Sadiq pour himself a drink and come to sit opposite her on a matching chair. The lights in the room made his amazing good-looks stand out. An awful alien yearning tugged low in her belly and she put down the drink and crossed her arms across her chest defensively.

Grimly he said, 'I'd forgotten all about the paparazzi. Of course I had no intention of putting you in that situation.'

Samia gulped, her anger dissipating. She knew he was telling the truth. A man like him would not have to resort to such measures. Restless, Samia stood up. 'Look, thank you for the dinner... I—'

She stopped when Sadiq stood too, and she had to curb the ridiculous urge to look for an exit, as if she were alone with a wild animal. Samia put out her hands wide in an unconsciously pleading gesture.

'What happened just now should prove how unsuitable I am. That was my first time being caught by the paparazzi. You need someone who is used to that kind of thing—who knows how to handle it.'

Distaste curdled in Sadiq's belly. That was exactly what he didn't want. He was more sure than ever that he wanted *her*—and for reasons that went beyond the practical and mundane.

He came closer to Samia and an unmistakable glint of triumph shone in his eyes and she felt sick. She could talk till she was blue in the face but the game was up. He'd called her bluff. She'd shown her telltale confusion. He'd manipulated her beautifully. Bitter recrimination burnt her. He was so close now that all she could see were those mesmerising eyes, and all she could smell was that uniquely male scent.

'Your reaction tells me you're conflicted about this decision, Samia. So let me take the conflict out of it for you. Agree to become my wife because there simply is no other alternative. You are of royal blood, from an ancient lineage. You were born for this role, and nothing you do or say can change that. To fight this is to fight fate, me and your brother.'

From his jacket pocket he pulled out a small velvet box, and all the while his eyes never left hers. He opened it, and Samia couldn't help but look down between them. The ring was surprisingly simple. It was obviously an antique—a square-cut stone in a gold setting, strikingly unusual and beautiful.

'It's a yellow sapphire. It was my paternal grandmother's—a gift from my grandfather on one of their wedding anniversaries.'

Sadiq didn't tell her that this distinctive ring had been

in his mind's eye ever since he'd met her, and that it was a lucky coincidence it had been in the family's jewel vault in London. He'd sent back the diamond ring he'd planned on using, feeling absurdly exposed in acknowledging that he hadn't been happy with a stock ring, which should have been perfectly adequate for what was essentially a stock wedding.

Samia looked up, and Sadiq took her hand in his. He looked so deep into her eyes that she felt as if she might drown and diappear for ever. She knew on some rational level that he was probably not even aware of his power. Unconsciously her fingers tightened around his as if to anchor herself, and something undefinable lit in Sadiq's eyes, hypnotising her even more.

'Princess Samia Binte Rashad al Abbas, will you please do me the very great honour of becoming my wife and Queen of Al-Omar?'

CHAPTER FOUR

AT that cataclysmic moment, while Sadiq's words hung in the air, Samia had a flashback she couldn't repress. She was hiding in the library of his castle after knocking over the table of drinks, cursing herself for being so clumsy and awkward. Her peace was shattered when a man walked into the room.

He didn't spot her because the lights were dim, and all Samia knew as she sat there barely breathing was that he was tall, dark and powerful looking. Yet she wasn't afraid. He walked over to the window which overlooked one of the castle's numerous beautiful inner courtyards and stood there for long moments, as silent as a statue, with an air of deep melancholy pervading the air around him.

He sighed deeply and dropped his head to run a weary hand back and forth over his short hair. Something about this man was connecting with Samia on a very deep level, she *felt* his pain, empathised with his isolation. Without even thinking about what she was doing, responding to some impulse to do *something*, Samia was almost out of her chair when another person entered the room: a woman, tall and blonde and statuesque, and very, very beautiful.

The man turned around and to Samia's shock she realised it was the charismatic Sultan she'd met only hours before. The melancholy and sense of isolation disappeared. She watched as his blue eyes glittered, taking in the woman's approach. In the place of the vulnerability she might have imagined was the hard shell of a supremely confident and sexual man, and she knew then that she had witnessed something incredibly private—something of himself that he would hate to know had been witnessed by anyone else.

Samia watched the woman walk straight up to him. She twined herself around him and, perversely, Samia wanted the Sultan to push this woman away contemptuously. As if he was hers! But as she watched, mesmerised, he backed the blond beauty up against a wall and proceeded to kiss her so passionately that Samia made an inadvertent sound of dismay.

Two faces turned towards her and Samia ran from the room, mortified to have been caught watching like a voyeur.

And now she was looking up into those same blue eyes, and she felt as if a hole had opened up in her belly. All she could remember was that intense vulnerability she'd seen, or *thought* she'd seen, in the Sultan that night, and the connection she'd felt.

She couldn't block out that image of the secret side of this man even as she sensed his steely determination. He would not rest until she said yes, and that made a curious sense of calm settle over her. He was right: to fight this was to fight fate, her brother and *him*. She denied to herself that that evocative memory was a tipping point, because that would mean that Sadiq was connecting with her on an emotional level, and she would deny that with every cell in her body.

This decision was about inevitability, logic and practicality, and the sheer weight of her lineage which put her in this position. She opened her mouth to speak and saw Sadiq's jaw tense, as if warding off a blow. Immediately she felt the impulse to reach up and smooth his jaw. She clenched her hand.

'I...' Her voice sounded rusty. 'Yes. I'll marry you.'

For a second there was no reaction. She wasn't even sure if she'd spoken out loud. But then Sadiq slid the ring onto her finger, bent his head and pressed his lips to it. They were warm and slightly parted, and her belly tightened with a need that was becoming horribly familiar. His head was so close to her breast...

He stood again and she saw that a shutter had come down over his expression, turning him aloof. He was the stern ruler again, and he had achieved his aim. No softness or charm now. Job done. Mission accomplished. Samia thought cynically of how he'd manipulated her emotions so beautifully. And yet she couldn't turn back now. She'd sealed her fate and chosen the path she would take for the rest of her life.

Her belly churning with the sudden realisation of what she'd just done, and a whole host of other scary emotions. She tried her best to match his dispassionate look and took her hand from his, stepping back. The ring twinkled and sparkled in her peripheral vision, and it was heavy. 'I've got to be up early, so if there's nothing else...?'

A ghost of a smile touched Sadiq's mouth and he too stepped back, letting Samia breathe a little easier. He shook his head. 'No, not right now. I'll have my assistant set up a schedule and send it over to you tomorrow. It's going to be a busy three weeks before we return to Al-Omar for our wedding.'

'Three weeks?' Samia squeaked, all pretence of insouciance gone at the terrifying thought. For some reason she'd imagined the wedding happening at some far-off distant time.

He nodded, all businesslike as he escorted her to the door. 'Three weeks, Samia. That should give you plenty of time to hand over your job and prepare for the wedding. I'll be in touch. There will be a press release issued next week. You might want to let your brother know the happy news before that happens.'

The following morning at work Samia finally found five minutes to steal away somewhere private and look at the tabloid she'd furtively bought on her way to the library. She held her breath as she took in the full glory of the lurid photo. She looked like a rabbit startled in the headlights, her eyes huge and her hair wild. And that suit! She could hear her stepmother's derisive voice in her head right now, exclaiming over Samia's general incompetence. She could have wept. Sadiq loomed behind her with a stern look on his gorgeous face, like an avenging dark angel, big hands on her waist making it look tiny. She looked more like an ill-dressed PA to the Sultan rather than his fiancée.

Fiancée. Her stomach churned as she crumpled up the offending paper. She'd left the engagement ring at home that morning and her skin prickled, as if somehow he would know and pop out from behind a corner to chastise her. She still couldn't really believe it, but a long conversation with her brother the previous night, and his palpable relief that they would have Al-Omar's cooperation, had helped reality sink in. It only eased her discomfort slightly.

The disturbing sense of equanimity that had washed over her when she'd said yes to Sadiq's proposal had long disappeared. It would be the wedding of the decade, and she would be annihilated when people realised she was nothing like his long line of mistresses. Not to mention the other aspects of their marriage—like the physical one. Samia felt a dart of despair. She was so far out of Sadiq's league in that respect that she fully expected he would have to take a mistress to stay satisfied.

The really galling thing was that she was as innocent and

pure as the virgin brides rulers like Sadiq would have expected for millenia. She'd had a bad experience in college when a boy who had been pursuing her had become very pushy after a couple of dates. Samia had turned his advances down and he'd stormed off, saying, *'I was only trying to get you into bed for a dare anyway, because of who you are, but I'm glad I didn't! Life is too short!'*

She'd repressed any hint of sexuality since then, not wanting to invite any cruel criticism or attention. Diverting her mind from the painful memory, she thought back to the phone call she'd received from Sadiq early that morning, just before she'd left for work.

'I've set up an appointment with a personal shopper this weekend. You'll need a trousseau. And wedding outfits. The festivities alone will last three days.'

Samia had sat down on the chair beside the phone, the future yawning open before her and looking scarier and scarier. 'Does it have to be three days? Why can't we just get married here in a civil ceremony with a couple of witnesses?'

He'd chuckled darkly and it had made Samia want to hit him. 'Because I'm a sultan and you're a princess about to become a queen, that's why. Also,' he'd continued briskly, 'you need to be protected. As of this morning you'll have two bodyguards, and you will be transported to and from work in one of my cars. The news may not be public yet, but enough people know, or suspect something.'

Samia's sense of personal freedom was disappearing fast, like an elusive shimmering oasis in the desert. 'But—' She'd started to protest, but had been cut off.

'That's non-negotiable. As of this moment you are under my protection. It's simply too dangerous for you to proceed as you have done. You're about to be married to one of the biggest fortunes in the world, not to mention the fact that you can also lay claim to one of the world's last remaining untapped oil bounties.'

At least, thought Samia with a hint of hysteria, she didn't have to worry that Sadiq was marrying her for her money! Any lingering sense of anonymity was a delicate thread about to break for ever.

Five days later

Sadiq was in the waiting area of one of the private dressing suites in London's most exclusive department store. Samia had been spirited away to somewhere within the labyrinthine rooms to be fitted out in a range of designer outfits, while he was waited upon hand and foot by a veritable army of beautiful women, all of whom were making their interest glaringly obvious.

The latest blonde offered him an array of newspapers and he picked one. She lingered far too long, causing Sadiq to bid her a curt thank-you. Once, not so long ago, he would have looked and decided if she was worth bedding. But not today, and never again.

That thought didn't fill him with the claustrophobia he might have expected. He had to admit that his resolve to stay faithful wasn't entirely down to the fact that he was about to be married but because curiosity and desire just weren't there.

He hadn't seen Samia again until he'd picked her up that morning. He'd told himself that he had to come with her because, after seeing her wardrobe, he couldn't trust that she would pick appropriate outfits. He conveniently ignored the fact that she'd been assigned a stylist with plenty of experience.

Samia had been waiting outside her apartment building, her hair tied back and looking pale and haunted in faded jeans, a light long-sleeved top and jacket. More unadorned than the servants who worked for him at the Hussein castle in B'harani. He'd had to quell irritation and also the disturbing flare of desire. Her jeans clung lovingly to slim legs and a pertly plump bottom. And the thin material of her top showed him again that her breasts were well shaped and more generous than he'd first assumed.

He'd reassured himself that his burgeoning desire for his fiancée was purely his head instructing his body to feel something for the only woman he would sleep with ever again, but the anticipation firing up his blood made a mockery of that assertion.

When he'd formally asked Samia to marry him after their dinner, he'd been overcome with a sense of desperation that she should agree—the first time he'd felt anything like it... or the first time in a long time. And he hadn't welcomed it.

A curious sense of fear tightened his body now, as he heard the whisper of movement which meant his fiancée was returning to parade the first of her outfits for his pleasure. He'd decided that Princess Samia would make him a good, uncomplicated wife, and suddenly the road ahead seemed paved with complications he'd not accounted for.

Samia wanted to yank the silver sheath excuse for a dress up over her bust and down over her knees, but was too intimidated by the personal shopper who reminded her painfully of her stepmother. Looking her up and down while she'd stood there in her plain underwear, she'd muttered something like, *'Well, there's not much we can do. You're too short for most of these dresses...'*

Battling back trepidation at the thought of being paraded in front of Sadiq like a slave girl at an auction, Samia fixed her gaze forward, determined not to see the undoubtedly disappointed expression on his face. She'd not even looked at herself in the numerous mirrors.

They emerged into the waiting room and Samia was aware of the big, powerful body lounging indolently on a cream sofa. Instantly her pulse quickened and that heat coiled low in her belly. She was teetering in sky-high heels and felt as unstable as a new foal on spindly legs.

Sadiq saw Samia emerge from behind a luxurious velvet curtain. He automatically raked her up and down with his eyes, as he had done with numerous women in the past—a reflex. This was usually an erotic prequel for their mutual pleasures later on. But never in his life had any of those women had this immediate an effect on him. So immediate and forcible that he had to angle his body in such a way as to disguise its rampant response.

Samia's hair was still tied back in a bun at the nape of her neck. He'd had to curb his urge to ask her to take it down earlier, as if she were his mistress and she wasn't pleasing him. Now she was avoiding his eye, and she was obviously excruciatingly embarrassed. He could see the telling red flush creep over her chest and up her neck and something inside him twisted.

But she was simply the most erotic vision he'd ever seen in his life. Far from his first impression of no curves, an almost boyish figure, she actually possessed the body of a houri. Without the boxy suits, jeans and unflattering top, she was all slender limbs and curves. He couldn't take his eyes off the full line of her bosom, like some kind of out-of-control teenager. Her skin looked silky-soft and pale golden, and he could imagine the contrast between his skin and hers as their limbs entwined. The acute ache in his groin intensified.

His voice came, low and authoritative. 'Leave us for a moment, please.'

To his relief the stylist and her assistants melted away.

Privacy was something he'd never had to worry about before, having always managed to stay in control. It was as if some invisible barrier had existed between him and women before, keeping them at some kind of a distance, but here with Samia…there was no barrier…just heat.

The dress was totally inappropriate, but it revealed the intoxicating combination of Samia's innocence and an earthy sexuality that she clearly had no clue she possessed. He didn't expect for a moment that she wasn't experienced, but he would bet right then that any lover she'd had hadn't awoken her sensuality, and a fiercely primitive feeling swept through him.

And then he realised that Samia was still resolutely avoiding his gaze. Her reluctance for this scenario was palpable. He had an uncomfortable flashback to the way his father had used to insist on his mother parading the latest fashions from Paris he'd bought for her. He knew this was nothing like that, but his desire was doused as effectively as if he'd stepped into a freezing cold shower.

His voice was arctic. 'That dress is entirely unsuitable. Clearly we've come to the wrong place. Go and change. We're leaving.'

Sadiq saw Samia's jaw tense, and the set of her shoulders as she turned and walked stiffly back through the curtain, and had to restrain himself from stopping her and explaining…*what?* That for a second he'd been afraid that he'd turned into his father? His overweight, overbearing father, who had flaunted his women in front of his only son as if it was something to be proud of, and in front of his stoic wife like a punishment for as long as Sadiq could remember?

Distaste curdled his insides, and he got up and paced impatiently while he waited for Samia.

At least he would never subject her to what his mother had had to endure for years, despite whatever justification his

father might have believed he had. Sadiq had always vowed
he would do things differently. He would have nothing but
respect for his wife and would treat his heirs like human be-
ings, not pawns.

Samia took a breath and stepped back into the main suite.
She was still stinging inside at Sadiq's cold condemnation of
the outfit—and *her*. She hadn't looked at him once but she
hadn't had to to know that his eyes had inspected every single piece of her and found it lacking. It had taken all of her
strength to stand there and endure it. Even her rejection at
the hands of that college boy was paling into insignificance
next to Sadiq's silent but damning appraisal.

She stepped back into the suite to see Sadiq looking so
broodingly at the floor that she had to battle the almost overwhelming feeling of *déjà vu* and curb the impulse to ask him
if anything was wrong. She almost laughed at herself. As
if she needed to ask! He was marrying *her*. And it was all
wrong—if only he would agree with her.

He turned to look at her and her hands gripped her jacket.
She felt shabby and more unsuitable then ever to be Queen.
'That dress—I don't think it—'

His hand slashed through the air. 'It did nothing for you
because it was far too obvious and your beauty is not obvious. It's subtle. Clearly this was the wrong place to come.
We'll have to go to Paris instead.'

Samia's mouth opened but nothing came out. She hadn't
known what he would say but she hadn't expected that. For
a moment her weak heart had fluttered to hear him describe
her as beautiful, but then the *subtle* had struck home. It was
just another way of saying she was plain.

Sadiq was already pacing away and speaking rapidly into
his phone in fluent French, taking her arm to hustle her out
of the suite and the shop. Anger was starting to bubble low

in her belly at his heavy-handed behaviour, but now he was on his third phone call and she could tell from the guttural Arabic that it was about politics in Al-Omar. Samia was used to her brother switching off and becoming impossible to deal with at times like this, so she just crossed her arms and seethed silently beside Sadiq.

Within an hour they were ascending into the clear blue sky from a private airfield in the middle of London. Samia wasn't unused to private air travel—her own family had a fleet of jets and helicopters—but she and her brother only used them when absolutely necessary. Both were keenly aware of the environment and their carbon footprint, and of wanting to set an example.

She wasn't aware that Sadiq had terminated his phone call until a drawling voice asked, 'Are you going to ignore me for the entire flight?'

Samia turned to face him, instantly cowed by how gorgeous he looked with his jacket off and his shirt open at the throat. She wanted to know what he would look like in jeans and a T-shirt.

Her wayward imaginings made her snap more caustically than she would have intended, 'I could ask the same of you. And I've told you all along how unsuitable I am, so I don't appreciate your silent, cold condemnation when I don't morph into the bride you want.'

His eyes narrowed on her. 'I meant what I said back there, Samia. I don't hand out platitudes or compliments for the sake of it. It's not my style. I simply recognised that the establishment I'd chosen was entirely wrong for you.' His eyes travelled up and down her body with leisurely appraisal, and then back to her face, which was hot. 'Like I said, your beauty is subtle and needs a more…delicate approach.'

Samia still refused to believe for a second that he really meant what he'd said. This was just his way of placating her.

And now he was taking her somewhere they could camouflage her better. Stiffly she said, 'Well, I hope it's worth the expense and environmental impact of taking a private plane all the way to Paris just to dress me.'

Dark amusement made his eyes glint and Samia's heart speed up.

'Don't worry, Princess. I can assure you that our carbon footprint will be as minimal as possible. One of my own team of scientists is using this plane as a vehicle to test out more environmentally friendly fuels. So, actually, we're providing valuable research.'

Samia refused to let his humour infect her. 'You really have an answer for everything, don't you?'

He smiled properly now, and it made him look ten years younger and less cynical. 'Of course.'

Samia had to turn away. He was far too attractive at that moment, and she feared that he'd see something of the ambiguous emotions she was feeling on her far too expressive face. That she found him attractive was undeniable, but that was just pure human reaction to one of the most virile specimens of man on the planet. She denied to herself that the attraction went any deeper than that—that what she felt went beyond the physical.

'Believe me,' he said now, 'when we announce our engagement to the press on Monday you'll be grateful for the armour of suitable clothing.'

'Monday…' Samia looked around, feeling herself pale. If there was any last moment when she could try and get out of this, it was now.

She was unaware of the wistful look on her face or the way Sadiq's tightened.

'Don't even think about it, Samia. We've gone too far to turn back now. There's already been speculation in the

papers after that photo. Now they're just waiting for an an-
nouncement.'

Her eyes narrowed on Sadiq and any hope was doused
at the steely look on his face. Bitterly she said, 'It's so easy
for you, isn't it? You've had your life of hedonistic freedom,
and now you've decided to marry it'll be executed with the
minimum of fuss and maximum haste.'

Sadiq's eyes flashed. 'You've had your freedom too,
Samia. As a modern twenty-five-year-old woman you can't
expect me to assume you've led such a nun's existence that
you're still a virgin?'

Instantly reacting to his mocking tone with a visceral need
to protect herself, Samia taunted, 'You mean you don't mind
that you won't be getting a pure wife on your wedding night?
I would have thought with the amount of care you put into
choosing your oh-so-suitable bride that it would have been
part of the checklist.'

Their gazes locked. Samia was breathing far too rapidly
for her liking. And she couldn't believe she'd more or less
lied so blatantly. She was leading him to believe she'd had
plenty of lovers.

A cynical smile curved Sadiq's sensual mouth. 'It doesn't
bother me in the least,' he drawled. 'Of course I didn't expect a pure bride. I'm not so old-fashioned or such a hypo-
crite. I've got a healthy sexual appetite and quite frankly the
thought of sleeping with a novice is not something I relish.'

A sudden pain lanced Samia. Ever since that experience
in college she'd locked away any romantic desire that she
would one day give herself to someone who would appreciate her for unique self. She'd told herself she didn't harbour
such dreams. And now she had to face the prospect of Sadiq's
horror when he found that he had indeed bagged himself an
innocent bride on their wedding night.

Overcome with an emotion she didn't want to analyse, and

feeling terribly vulnerable, Samia scrambled inelegantly out of her seat. She felt permanently inelegant next to this man. Muttering something about being tired, she escaped to the back of the cabin, where she'd been shown a bedroom earlier, and firmly closed the door behind her. They'd be landing soon, but Samia curled up on the bed anyway and tried to block out the taunting and gorgeous face of Sadiq in her mind's eye. She wondered how on earth she'd ever been deluded enough to think he might be vulnerable.

Sadiq flung down his phone and glared out of the small oval window of the plane. All he could see were clouds upon clouds—and Samia's face, with those big wounded aquamarine eyes shimmering more blue than green against the pale skin of her face. He had already come to notice how her eyes went dark blue when she was emotional.

She'd looked close to tears just then, but he couldn't fathom what he'd said to upset her. His mouth twisted wryly. Apart from asking her to marry him. He hadn't had such a comprehensive attack on his ego ever...and he had to acknowledge at the same time that it wasn't altogether unwelcome. Being surrounded by yes people and sycophants became wearing after a while.

He thought back to what he'd said, and still couldn't see that he'd said anything untoward. Of course he hadn't expected her to be pure and untainted. He was a modern man and a modern ruler. Why would he behave one way himself and expect his wife to have lived like a nun? The important thing was that, whatever Samia had been doing, he'd seen no evidence of it.

He gritted his jaw against the pervasive memory that threatened to burst free when he thought of the words *pure* and *untainted*. A woman had said those words to him with a scathing voice a long time ago.

Analia Medena-Gonzalez. A stunningly beautiful social-ite from Europe who had come to visit Al-Omar with her ambassador father when Sadiq had been eighteen. He'd been no innocent youth then, but he hadn't exactly been experi-enced either.

Analia, who was ten years his senior, had seduced him and reduced him to putty in her hands, enslaving him with the power of her sensuality and sexuality. And Sadiq, like the young fool he'd been, had believed himself in love with her.

She'd stood in front of him the day she was leaving and looked at him as if he'd just crawled out from under a rock. 'You *love* me? Sadiq, darling, you don't love me. You are in lust with me, that's all.'

Sadiq could remember biting back the words trembling on his lips to contradict her. Even then some self-preserving instinct had kicked in—much to his everlasting gratitude.

She'd looked him up and down with those exotic green eyes and sighed. 'Darling, I'm twenty-eight and looking for my second husband. You're still a boy. The sooner you learn to harden your heart and not fall for every woman you sleep with, the better it will be for you. I know the kind of women you'll meet. They will all want your body, yes, but they will also want you because you're powerful and rich. Two of the greatest aphrodisiacs.'

She'd come close then, and all but whispered into his ear, 'Believe me, Sadiq, they won't care about the man you re-ally are—just as I don't really care. That's why you have a mother. One day you'll choose some pure and untainted local girl to be your wife, and you'll live happily ever after.'

The banal cruelty of those words hadn't had the power to shock or hurt Sadiq for a long, long time. He'd learnt a valu-able lesson, and her prophecy had turned out to be largely true.

Once he'd become Sultan on his father's death, at the age

of nineteen, he'd been catapulted to another stratosphere. For almost a year Sadiq hadn't even taken a lover, too intent on taking control of a wildly corrupted and chaotic country. But once he'd re-emerged into society women had surrounded him in droves.

He'd quickly become an expert at picking the ones who knew how he wanted to play the game. No emotional entanglement, no strings. He'd become used to seeing the glazed, avaricious glitter in their eyes when they saw the extent of his inestimable wealth and on some perverse level it had comforted him—because he never again wanted to be standing in front of a woman laying himself bare to her pity and ridicule.

He'd actually met Analia once or twice over the years, and once had even seduced her again, as if to purge the effect of that day from his mind and heart for ever. He'd looked at her as she'd dressed the next morning and hadn't felt a thing. Not a twinge of emotion. It had been a small moment of personal triumph.

Seeing the way his father had been so pathologically enraged because his wife didn't love him should have been enough of a lesson to Sadiq, but it hadn't. He wasn't about to forget either of those valuable lessons now, just because the woman he'd chosen to marry was singularly unimpressed with everything he put before her, wore her vulnerability on her sleeve and made him feel unaccountably protective.

Samia was facing another velvet drape in another exclusive shop about three hours later—albeit this time in a secluded side street in Paris, the centre of world fashion. She'd woken just before the air stewardess had come to tell her they were about to land, and Sadiq had largely ignored her on the journey into Paris. She fiddled for a moment with the chiffon overlay of the dress, and then the much friendlier French stylist appeared at her side and tugged her through the drape. 'Come on, *chérie*. We have a lot of outfits to get through.'

Samia closed her eyes for a split second and held her breath, the bright light blinding her for a moment so she couldn't see the initial expression on Sadiq's face. He was standing near the window and he lowered the ever-present smart phone from his ear.

Samia desperately felt like fidgeting in the long dress, but the stylist was already fussing around her, tweaking and pulling. Resolutely refusing to be intimidated this time, she hitched up her chin and looked straight at Sadiq—but his gaze was somewhere around her breasts. Samia's jaw clenched; he was looking *for* them, no doubt. Although she had to admit that even she'd been surprised at how voluptuous the dress made them look.

The sylist had chided her that she'd been wearing the wrong size bra for years and had quoted a size of 32C, which had had Samia protesting vociferously that she must be wrong. Until she'd given her a bra to try and it had fitted like a second skin.

Sadiq's gaze finally ascended and his face was completely expressionless. Samia thought she saw a flare of something in those blue depths, but put it down to the light and cursed the traitorous jump in her pulse.

'Much better.' His voice was cool. 'This is more like it. Well done, Simone. Keep going.'

And then Samia was whisked away, back into the dressing room, and pushed and pulled and contorted into a dizzying array of outfits. Evening wear, daywear, casual wear, beachwear. She soon affected her own uninterest as she was paraded in front of Sadiq for the umpteenth time. And then they were finished. When she went back outside Sadiq was gone, and she felt an ominous lurch where her heart was.

She whirled around when the petite Frenchwoman appeared holding out her coat. 'Um…do you know where…?'

Simone smiled and said cheerily, in her gorgeous accent, 'Your fiancé is trusting my judgement for the rest of the day. You don't really want him to see your wedding outfits before the wedding, do you? And also…' She linked her arm with Samia who felt extremely uncomfortable—never having been a *girly* girl. 'I think when he sees you in your new underwear it should be a nice surprise, *non*?'

For the next few hours, until dusk fell over Paris, Samia endured the humiliation of having an army of women parade around her, poking and prodding, and of climbing in and out of underwear so indecently flimsy that she had no earthly intention of ever wearing it for herself, never mind for someone else!

She'd been measured for her main wedding dress, which she would wear on the final day of the celebrations—the most westernised part of the wedding. The rest of the fitting for that would take place the next day, as well as her spending a few hours in a beauty salon. In a couple of weeks the dress would be brought to London for a final fitting and last adjustments before they left for Al-Omar.

So apparently they were staying in Paris for the night. An ominous fluttering started up in Samia's belly.

Simone escorted her out to the car that had been ferrying them around all afternoon and bade her goodnight, telling her that all of the clothes would be delivered to London and then on to Al-Omar. She pressed a small luxury holdall into Samia's hands and winked. 'You might need this tonight.'

Samia wasn't sure what she meant until she opened it in the privacy of the back of the car. She had no idea where she was going, and was too tired to ask, and yet felt bizarrely secure in the knowledge that Sadiq would know exactly where she was.

And then she saw what was in the bag: a selection of silky underwear and pyjamas. There was a smaller bag, with exquisite toiletries and a change of clothes for the next day. She'd lost her own favourite jeans somewhere along the way today, and was now wearing a beautifully tailored pair of designer trousers and an indecently soft cashmere jumper. Together with the new lace bra she wore underneath it all felt far too decadent, and not *her*.

By the time the car pulled up outside a very expensive looking townhouse, with the iconic Al-Omar flag flying at the entrance, Samia was feeling decidedly prickly.

CHAPTER FIVE

SAMIA walked into a hushed, dimly lit and luxurious reception hall. A huge chandelier twinkled above her and a massive winding staircase led upwards. There were exquisite oriental rugs on polished parquet floors, and small antique tables with Chinese vases which she guessed were Ming. Delicate rococco design was everywhere, and expensive looking art on the walls. One of the bodyguards closed the main door behind her softly and Samia put her leather bag down, forgetting all about her discomfort in the face of this sheer opulence.

She took a moment drinking it in before she realised that Sadiq was lounging against a wall nearby, hands in pockets, half hidden in the gloom like some dark knight. Samia put her hand to her suddenly pounding heart, knowing that it had more to do with the immediate kick of her pulse at the sight of that powerful body than fright.

That prickliness was back. 'You scared me half to death. Do you normally sneak up on people like that?'

Sadiq pushed himself off the wall and strolled towards her, half coming into the light, so his face was all dark shadows and hard planes, his white shirt making those blue eyes pop out. 'I came back to take care of some work in the office, but I left you in good hands.' His eyes flicked down and Samia felt it almost like the faint lash of a whip. 'The clothes suit you…we should have come to Simone in the first place.'

His tone of voice, as if he was talking about an inanimate object, made Samia irrationally angry. Her hands were clenched. 'My jeans are gone. I liked those jeans. Do you know how long it takes to break in a pair of jeans? And my top and jacket…they were perfectly good. How can I go for a walk in Hyde Park in *these*?'

She stuck her foot out to indicate the beautiful but impractical soft leather ankle boots with high heels. Sadiq came closer and Samia stumbled backwards, off balance for a second.

'I'm afraid your days of walking in Hyde Park unaccompanied are gone, Samia. Do you want to tell me what's really wrong? You must be the only woman on this earth who can spend the day shopping with an unlimited credit card and not emerge from the experience ecstatic with joy.'

Samia diverted her gaze, suddenly ashamed at her petulance. 'I'm sorry. I don't mean to sound ungrateful…but it's just not *me*.' She plucked at the luxurious jumper which clung so lovingly to her body and looked back up, unaware of the beseeching look on her face. 'I was never into this sort of thing. I feel like…I don't know who I am any more. I'm losing myself.'

To Samia's surprise, Sadiq came and put his hands on her shoulders and propelled her gently but firmly to a long mirror on a panel of the wall nearby. He stood her in front of it. Immediately she saw her reflection and Samia winced and looked away, but Sadiq held her fast.

'Look at yourself, Samia.'

She screwed her eyes shut and shook her head. She'd managed to avoid it so far. Too many memories of her stepmother standing her in front of a mirror and pointing out all of her failings were threatening to swamp her. She'd never felt so vulnerable. Especially with Sadiq's big warm hands on her shoulders, sending all sorts of shockwaves down her arms and between her legs where a pulse throbbed. She could feel her breasts grow heavy, and the lace bra chafed against suddenly stinging nipples.

Oh, God.

'Open your eyes, Samia. We're not moving till you do.' Recognising that steel tone, Samia knew she had no choice. With the utmost reluctance she opened her eyes and then heard a dry, 'Now, look in the mirror.'

Why was it that *this* man was the one person who seemed to have been given the unique ability to make herself face up to all her innermost demons? She'd only known him for a week, and yet he already knew more about her than anyone else. Thanks to her futile attempts to persuade him that she wasn't suitable for him which had backfired in spectacular fashion.

She turned her head and looked defiantly into the blue eyes in the dark face above hers. The heels lessened the height difference between them, but it was still substantial. He was a whole head and shoulders above her.

Sadiq arched a brow. 'You can gaze into my eyes all you want, Samia, but the object of this exercise is for you to look at *yourself.*' He smiled, and it was mocking. 'However, if you would prefer to look at me, then…'

Her face flaming, Samia quickly diverted her gaze and looked at herself—because right now that was the lesser of two evils. Somewhere along the way her hair had come down and she'd lost her clip, so now it lay in long wavy tendrils over her shoulders and down her back. The little curly pieces she could never control were framing her face. Her hair had been down more often in the past week than it had since she'd been a child. Her eyes were glittering almost feverishly in her too-pale face, with two bright spots of pink in her cheeks. She groaned inwardly; she looked as if she'd just been picking apples off a tree in an orchard. About as unsophisticated as you could possibly get.

And then she saw where the clinging material of her jumper moulded lovingly to her breasts, which suddenly seemed huge, the hard points of her nipples clearly pushing against the fabric. This should have been the point when she pulled away, made some facetious comment and broke the tension. But a heavy langour seemed to have invaded her veins, a curious lethargy, and yet there was an energy too, fizzing and jumping in her blood.

The trousers lay flat against her pelvis and then skimmed her legs, elongating them and making them look almost slender.

Sadiq's voice sounded rough, and his hands tightened marginally on her shoulders. 'Perhaps, Samia, it's about you finding yourself, *not* losing yourself at all. The image in that mirror is one of a woman who is about to become a queen, and the sooner you can see that too, the better. I can see it, so you really shouldn't doubt yourself.'

His hands were suddenly gone, and so was the warmth from his body behind her. She turned around and saw he was walking away, throwing over his shoulder carelessly, 'Helene will show you to your room. We'll eat in an hour.'

As if by magic a small wizened woman appeared and beckoned with a smile for Samia to follow her. She already had her bag in her hand. Sadiq's words about finding herself were ringing in her ears and affecting her at a very visceral level as she followed the housekeeper.

Sadiq closed the door behind him in his huge study and leant back against it for a moment, shutting his eyes. But it was no good. All he could see was the provocative fullness of Samia's breasts pushing against that flimsy top. They weren't even clothes designed to drive a man wild with desire! What would he do when she appeared in the long strapless evening dress she'd worn earlier, which had pushed the pale swells of her breasts high above the bodice?

When Samia had disappeared for another change he'd made a fool of himself by asking Simone tersely if it was entirely appropriate for any kind of function they'd be attending, and Simone had looked at him with dry amusement. '*Chéri*, that dress alone contains about three hundred more yards of material than the excuse for a dress you bought the last time you were here—so, yes, it's fine.'

His eyes snapped open again but that image of Samia— one long slender leg revealed in a thigh-high slit, bare shoulders and that enticing cleavage—was burned onto his retinas. He went and poured himself a shot of whisky and walked to the window, which looked out over the immaculate flood-lit gardens. How long had she been keeping that body hidden under those boxy suits? All her life, he'd guess, and yet for all of her apparent shyness and insecurity he was seeing more and more tantalising flashes of something much more feisty.

It had been some kind of torture today, watching her parade in front of him in a range of outfits. And he couldn't fathom it. He'd watched women parade in front of him for years and it had never had such a profound effect on him.

But with each successive fitting today Sadiq's tension had risen and risen, to the point that he'd had to leave or turn into a slavering fool in front of the impeccably cool Simone, whom he suspected had already noticed the change in his usually unflappable demeanour.

The wedding dress and underwear fittings had not come soon enough, and he'd all but run out of the salon. And now he stood here, hand clenched around his glass, wondering why he felt so threatened at facing the unexpected reality that he desired his wife-to-be. Surely this had to be a *good* thing? His wedding night would be no hardship.

Even at that thought his body hardened, and Sadiq cursed. He was reduced to being turned on—as if someone was controlling a remote mechanism from a distance! He took a deep gulp of the drink and winced slightly, chastising himself. He had nothing to fear. He was being ridiculous. It was as simple as this: he was embarking on an arranged marriage and his head was merely telling his body that he desired his wife. Biology, pure and simple, to ensure that he sired heirs.

Nevertheless, when Sadiq sat down and tried to concentrate on important correspondence trepidation skated over his nerve-endings.

A little later Sadiq sat back in his chair and twirled a wine glass in his hands, the ruby liquid catching the light. Samia was mesmerised by the play of muscles in Sadiq's forearm and had to force herself to remember what he'd just asked.

'My father remarried when I turned two. Alesha was a distant cousin of his, from the northern territory of Burquat.'

Sadiq's eyes narrowed on Samia and she looked down to her empty dessert plate.

'That's it?'

Samia shrugged minutely, uncomfortably aware of how the material of her top skated over her suddenly sensitive skin. 'She wasn't...very maternal. I think she viewed my brother and I as a threat.' She looked up at Sadiq again and tried a wry smile. 'You see, my father truly loved our mother, even though it had been an arranged marriage. And when she died...' Samia's smile faltered when she thought of the deep wells of sadness her father's eyes had been. 'He was devastated.'

Sadiq frowned. 'You said she died in childbirth with you?'

Samia nodded and swallowed, pushing down the emotion

she always thought she had no right to feel—that yawning sense of loss. 'She developed pre-eclampsia and by the time they realised why she'd gone into labour early it was too late. She slipped into a coma and died a few days later.'

Wanting to divert the attention from herself, Samia asked, 'You never had any brothers or sisters?'

He looked up, and the sudden tension in the air and in Sadiq's face warned Samia that she had strayed into sensitive territory—which made her curious.

He shook his head. 'No. Just me.' He smiled, but it was tight, and drained the last of his wine.

She'd obviously touched a nerve and was instantly intrigued. She watched the strong column of his throat work, and then flushed when she realised that he had put the glass down and was looking at her intently. Her scalp itched where a few strands of hair were pulled too tight. She'd put it up again, but instead of feeling more comfortable, it actually made her feel self-conscious.

Before she knew what was happening Sadiq had reached across the table and taken her hand in his. She couldn't pull away, and just watched dumbly as he turned it over in his palm. It looked tiny and very white cradled in his. And then he intertwined his fingers with hers, and Samia felt a pulse throb between her legs. She pressed them tight together and desperately wished for him to release her.

As if he knew exactly what effect he was having on her Sadiq smiled. 'I believe this will work, Samia. A marriage between us. You underestimate your appeal, you know.'

Her eyes met his and she bit her lip. She thought of the cool way he'd looked at her in countless different outfits all day, as if she were a brood mare. He was making her feel all hot and bothered, and sudden anger at his easy charm made her snap, 'You mean I should be grateful that you don't find me so repulsive that you won't need to be blindfolded to take me to bed on our wedding night?'

He smiled again, and it sent Samia's blood pounding through her body.

'On the contrary, Princess Samia. I think we'll be lucky if we make it to our wedding night without sleeping together. After all, we're both adults, both experienced, and I think we've established that neither one of us is bound by such romantic ideals as waiting till the night of our wedding. Introducing a blindfold into the proceedings certainly might add a little...something... But it won't be for me. I want to see every reaction that crosses your expressive face when we sleep together for the first time.'

A million things exploded in Samia's head at once, even as she registered that Sadiq's thumb was now stroking lazily across her hectic pulse point. But superseding everything was the thought of all that potent masculinity focused solely on her. It was overwhelming.

Not thinking clearly at all, beyond escaping the sudden threat he posed, Samia pulled her hand free of Sadiq and said priggishly, 'Well, I quite like the idea of adhering to tradition.'

Sadiq sat back again, and Samia wondered how someone could appear to be so relaxed and yet threatening at the same time. A dark shadow of stubble made the line of his jaw seem even harder, more defined, and the deepset blue eyes over the slightly hawklike nose should have given him a cruel aspect, but instead it all added up to one of the most beautiful faces she'd ever seen on a man. And that was including her brother, who seemed to turn any woman he encountered into a simpering bimbo.

His lower lip alone was indecent in its sensual provocation. When he spoke his voice was throaty. 'I think you're a tease, Samia. You say one thing and then you look at me as if you want to climb over this table and devour me whole. Is this what you do? Present men with an innocent, slightly gauche exterior and then reveal yourself bit by bit until they're begging for mercy?'

Her face truly flaming now, Samia looked at Sadiq. He had no idea. She was reacting to him because he was the first man who had broken through the thin veneer of control she'd believed impermeable for so long. *He* was the reason she was unravelling at the seams and revealing anything of her inner self.

She shook her head. 'I'm not teasing. Trust me.'

His face was suddenly all harsh lines and angles. 'So that little performance out there in front of the mirror was real? Are you going to tell me who was the one who made you so averse to looking at your own reflection?'

Ice entered Samia's veins. He was digging too deep, too fast. 'I don't know what you're talking about.' She felt as if her skin was being pulled back so all of her insecurities were laid bare. 'I wouldn't know how to tease my way out of a paper bag, and I never could act.'

She stood up with as much grace as she could muster and watched the way his eyes dropped to the level of her breasts before returning slowly to her face. *You're the tease!* She wanted to shout at him.

'It's been a long day, so if you don't mind I'll retire for the night.' *Brilliant. Now she sounded like a Victorian heroine.*

Sadiq stood too, and inclined his head. He looked huge on the other side of the table. 'By all means—be my guest. The car will pick you up at 10:00 a.m. tomorrow. I'm afraid I won't be here for breakfast as I've got an important conference call to take with my ministers in the morning. It'll run into a few hours. But I'll see you for dinner tomorrow evening.'

* * *

The following day Samia was grateful for the chance to lie horizontal while she had her eyelashes tinted. She'd hardly slept a wink after that conversation with Sadiq, and now she'd had the wedding dress fitting and had then deposited in this opluent beauty salon just off the Champs-Elysées, with Simone issuing a stream of incomprehensible instructions to the team of therapists assigned to her. For someone who'd never had a facial or a massage in her life, the whole experience was a little scary—if faintly pleasurable.

She wondered how many of his women had been brought to the same place, and couldn't stop a dart of something that felt awfully like jealousy from spiking in the pit of her belly.

One day in the library last week, when the others had been on a lunch break, Samia—much to her everlasting shame— had looked up archived newspaper reports about Sadiq. Of all of the women with whom he'd been associated just one name had popped up more than once, and it belonged to a well-known and beautiful European socialite. Their on/ off affair seemed to stretch back to when Sadiq had been quite young, and immediately warning bells had gone off in Samia's head.

She'd witnessed her own brother change for ever and become hard after a love affair gone wrong when he was nineteen. She knew exactly how men like her brother and Sadiq could shut themselves off after feeling exposed. That memory of Sadiq in the library of the Hussein castle had taken on new significance.

A relatively recent photo of Sadiq with the same woman had said more than words ever could. They were entering an exclusive hotel in Paris and Sadiq was looking down into her perfect face. The intensity of his expression alone told Samia that if this man had once had a heart, it was long lost by now.

That evening, after their dinner had been cleared away, Samia looked at Sadiq and tried not to notice the fact that he looked tired.

In a bid to distract him from sensing her concern, she blurted out, 'How will this marriage be?' He frowned slightly, and Samia cursed herself. 'What I mean is...are you going to keep mistresses on the side?' She stuck out her chin. 'Because I won't stand for that. I won't be publicly ridiculed.'

Samia was surprised at the vehemence in her voice. Clearly she'd gone from assuming he would have to take a lover to stay satisfied to rejecting the notion with every cell in her body. The picture of him with that woman was burning a hole in her brain.

Sadiq smiled, and it was mocking enough to make Samia want to slap him.

'First of all, I've never had *mistresses*. I'm a one-woman man. At a time.'

Samia cringed. 'You know what I mean.'

'I don't currently have a mistress, as I would see it as incredibly bad taste to get engaged while entertaining another woman. And, contrary to what some people may expect— clearly all the gossips *you* were listening to—I have every intention of being a faithful husband.'

Samia flushed and said defensively. 'I wasn't listening to gossips... It's not exactly a secret that you've had plenty of...lovers.'

A look of distaste flashed across Sadiq's face. 'My own father paraded his mistresses in front of my mother, and I always vowed not to disrespect a wife like that. It turned my mother into a recluse.'

A wife. So impersonal. Did he regard her as just *a wife*? As if she even needed that question answered. Of course he did. And why did that suddenly not feel okay to her?

Wanting to avoid that line of questions and answers, she asked, 'You didn't get on with your father?'

Sadiq's mouth twisted and he looked at her coolly, some

indefinable emotion flashing across his face. 'Not exactly, no. He was an angry man for much of the time, for various reasons. And he took that anger out on my mother—and me—when it suited him.'

Samia had an immediate sense of a small boy being neglected and hated, and her heart contracted at that image. She wondered if that anger had ever turned physical. She'd got used to avoiding her stepmother's free hands and could sense that Sadiq too had become adept at getting out of harm's way. This hint of vulnerability was making all sorts of flutters take off in Samia's belly, and she longed to ask him more, but couldn't. He was already looking as if he regretted saying anything, and she was just beginning to realise how little he revealed of himself at all.

'Does your mother live with you?'

Sadiq nodded. 'She has her own quarters in the castle. You'll meet her when you come to B'harani before the wedding to settle in.'

Samia's belly tensed. Her eyes darted away from his intense gaze. That blue that seemed to sear right through her. She fiddled with the ring on her wedding finger, unused to its heavy weight.

'What if...?' She trailed off. What Samia really wanted to ask was what if she didn't please him in bed? How could he honestly say then that he wouldn't take a mistress? But instead she said, 'What if we have problems with children... getting pregnant?'

'Then I would divorce you and marry again.'

The speed of his response and its stark finality made Samia look at him again. Her mouth opened and shut. She was not sure at all how she felt about that, and was not liking the feeling. Finally she got out, 'What if it's *you* that has the problem?'

He smiled tightly. 'It won't be me.'

His insufferable arrogance made Samia sit up straight in her seat. 'Well, of course it could be you. Not even you can tell the future. You might be the Sultan but—'

'I *know*.' He cut her off. 'I've had medical tests and there's no evidence that there should be problems.'

Samia's mouth closed. 'But...why would you doubt your ability to have children?'

Sadiq sat back in his seat and a muscle twitched in his jaw. 'When you tell me who it was that nurtured your lack of confidence, and why you can't look at yourself in the mirror, then I'll tell you why I believed it necessary to get checked out.'

Stalemate. No way was Samia going to open herself up to his pity and mockery.

He was grim. 'I didn't think so.' He stood up then and loomed tall across the table. 'I have business to attend to in my study, if you'll excuse me?'

Samia half stood too, her mind whirling. He sounded accusatory, as if angry with her for bringing up these issues. 'Of course...'

He stopped at the door and turned back. 'When we arrive in London in the morning we're going to give a press conference to announce the marriage, so wear something suitable.' His mouth quirked as he obviously saw the terror dawn on Samia's face. 'Don't worry. I'll do the talking. You just have to stand there and look like you're not walking the plank.'

As they stood in front of the world's media the next morning, Sadiq's arm was tight around Samia's waist. She was tucked in to his side and tense enough to crack. Cameras flashed and questions were hurled out in about five different languages. Sadiq of course replied in kind, and with him by her side, she had to admit that this wasn't half as scary as she'd feared.

She'd be eternally grateful that Simone had called to the house that morning to drop off some photos of suggestions for accessories for the wedding. She had helped Samia pick out an outfit, and now she was wearing a plain shift dress in dark blue with a matching jacket.

Her hair was down after Sadiq had given her an express look on the private jet and said succintly, 'Either you take it down, or I will. The hairdresser was told to leave it alone for a reason.'

To her utter relief Samia heard Sadiq announce that he would take a final question, and then a cheeky Cockney voice piped up from the back. 'Give her a kiss, will you?'

Samia hadn't really registered what he'd said until she was being turned into Sadiq's body and his hands were on her arms. He was smiling down at her, a sardonic expression on his face. 'They're looking for a public display of affection—think you can manage it?'

Samia gulped and wanted to shake her head and say no, because suddenly standing in front of a baying pack of newshounds was far less threatening than the fact that Sadiq's head was coming closer and closer and she couldn't move.

In that moment Sadiq thought how ironic it was as someone who'd never previously relished any kind of PDA, he found that he couldn't wait to kiss this woman, despite the wall of media just feet away. He pulled her into his body and knew that surprise was making her more malleable. She felt so delicate, so *small*, and instinctively he curved around her as if to protect her. She was looking up at him like a deer caught in the headlights, eyes huge.

Anticipation lasered through his veins like a shot of adrenalin, and the first taste of her mouth against his was so impossibly sweet that he groaned softly. Her lips were as soft as he'd imagined they would be. The room and all the people faded into the background as he slid his arms around her back to arch her into him even more.

He felt her hands cling on to the lapels of his jacket, but he was drowning in the sweet nectar of possibly one of the most chaste kisses he'd ever experienced. It was having anything but a chaste effect on his body—especially when he could feel the firm swells of Samia's breasts pressed into his chest.

Everything was tightening and hardening, and he knew he had to stop and pull back, try and regain some sanity. But just at that moment Samia opened her mouth. He felt the tentative touch of her tongue to his and his brain went red-hot.

It was a long second before Samia realised that Sadiq had stopped kissing her and was practically pushing her back from him, hands on her arms. She felt dizzy and disorientated and her lips were tingling. Catcalls and whistles brought her back to earth, though, and with her face flaming she let Sadiq usher her off the temporary dais and out to the waiting car. Her legs were wobbly and she prayed she would stay upright.

He handed her in to the car, but didn't follow. He was stooping at the door, looking in, and Samia felt bewildered and curiously emotional. It was as if an earthquake had just happened. But Sadiq looked so cool she wondered for a minute if they had even kissed.

His voice was as cool as he looked. 'I'm staying here to take a flight to Al-Omar. I have to return to take care of government business—I've been gone too long. You'll be well protected in the meantime, and I'll see you in two weeks.'

Samia looked at the harshly beautiful face, the pristine suit and tie, her eyes glittering. Every inch of him was the stupendously powerful ruler who had taken care of sorting out a convenient wife. He'd come into her life like a whirlwind,

upending everything, and now he was leaving just as suddenly.

To avoid having him see the sudden confusion she was
feeling written all over her face, she said, 'Okay...' and
turned to face the front. As if she was absolutely unmoved
by that kiss, and not feeling suspiciously *bereft*!

'I trust you'll have enough time to get your affairs in
order?'

Samia swallowed back the lurch of emotion that came
from somewhere scary. He was making it sound as if she
was going to die. And *was* she going to die a kind of death?
Even as she thought that she could feel the blood pumping
through her veins, making a mockery of her thoughts. She'd
never felt *more* alive than in this moment. Not even when
she'd battled the ocean on that boat.

Aware of Sadiq waiting for a response, she vigorously
nodded her head. 'Yes. It'll be fine.' She just wanted to be
gone—away from his intense regard and those all-seeing
eyes.

After an infinitesimal moment the door shut, and then
the car was moving and she was being driven away from
the tall figure. Samia didn't turn around to look at Sadiq, so
she didn't see how long he stood there—long after the car
had disappeared.

The shockwave that had gone through her body when
Sadiq's mouth had touched hers was still there. His effect
on her had been nothing short of cataclysmic, but she could
imagine just how mind-numbingly unerotic that kiss must
have been for him. How could it have been anything else?
She remembered the way it had taken her a second to come
to her senses, only to realise that he was all but prising her
off him. And in front of the world's media.

Samia's emotions were all over the place. Up till now
they'd been pretty straightforward: she had agreed to this

marriage because quite simply she knew she had a responsibility and a destiny to fulfil. Except now…something had shifted inside her. Something had given way, and in its place were *emotions* and feelings. And that kiss hadn't helped one bit. It had put those emotions right to the forefront. The kiss had made the desire she'd been trying to deny rise up, and now it would not be suppressed again.

In the past couple of days she'd seen chinks in the cool armour the Sultan wore so well. It had been easy to think of him as just a ruthless, cynical man, determined to get his own way. But she now knew—or at least suspected— that he'd once been in love. She knew that he'd had a less than perfect relationship with his father. He'd grown up alone, with no brothers or sisters. Despite the pain her stepmother had caused her, Samia wouldn't have survived without her brother and sisters.

She couldn't stop an image forming in her head of a small dark haired toddler running into Sadiq's arms, and put a hand to her mouth in shock at her wayward imagination—and, worse, the yearning feeling that accompanied it. She'd never thought of herself as maternal, and it would be emotional suicide to harbour such fantasies when marrying someone who would only see children as *heirs* and *spares*. Sadiq hadn't said as much, but he hadn't said anything, either, to discount that view.

Samia groaned softly, and jumped when the driver asked, 'Is everything all right, Your Highness?'

She got out a garbled yes, and resolutely pushed aside her disturbing line of thinking. She had to concentrate on packing up her life here in London. Movers would be taking most of her stuff to Sadiq's London home, and the rest would be shipped to Al-Omar. In two weeks she'd be meeting her fiancé again in her new home, and her life would change for ever. But that wasn't half as daunting as the prospect of seeing Sadiq again.

CHAPTER SIX

By the end of the third day in B'harani, two weeks later, Samia knew she needn't have worried about how seeing Sadiq would affect her because he'd spent a grand total of five minutes with her.

The day she'd arrived she'd been looking around the extensive and luxurious surroundings of her private suite of rooms when a peremptory knock had come on the door. Without waiting for an answer someone had opened it. Samia's crazy heartbeat had told her that it could only be one person, as everyone else had been deferential to the point of embarrassment.

Sadiq had swept into the room, dominating the entire space immediately, resplendent in traditional white and gold Al-Omari robes. And even though she'd grown up seeing men in traditional dress he'd still taken her breath away. There had been something intensely masterful about the image he'd presented.

He'd been brusque and short, blue eyes disturbingly intense. 'I trust you had a good journey and that your rooms are to your liking?'

Samia had nodded, her mouth dry, tongue-tied in the face of his overwhelming presence and sheer masculinity. And this cool reception.

'Everything was...*is* fine. Thank you.'

'Good. I'm afraid I won't have much free time to spend with you as I'm trying to clear my schedule for the wedding and honeymoon.'

He had looked tired, dark stubble lining his jaw, and absurdly concern had risen within Samia. She had shrugged lightly, suddenly relieved that she wouldn't be the focus of his attention straight away, while trying not to think about his reference to the *honeymoon*. 'That's fine. I understand.'

He'd cracked a small tight smile and then said, with a rough quality to his voice that had resonated deep within her, 'You don't have to look so pleased to see the back of me. I'll make sure you're given tours of the castle and one of my aides will show you around B'harani. We have a public function to attend on Thursday night, before the wedding festivities start at the weekend. By Sunday we will be man and wife, and you will be Queen.'

The memory died away. Samia had just returned to her room after having dinner with Sadiq's mother, Yasmeena. She'd been kind enough to take her under her wing, and Samia had seen from where Sadiq had inherited his unusual blue eyes. The elegant older woman had shown her around the castle. She was friendly, if a little reserved, and carried an air of deep sadness that reminded Samia poignantly of her father.

Responding to the allure of the dusky view outside her patio doors now, she went out to the private terrace which also held a small lap pool, complete with a kaleidescope of coloured mosaics, and walked across to the trellised wall. The balmy heat caressed her skin like a silken touch, and Samia realised just how much she'd missed this: the heat and the open spaces and the huge sky twinkling with stars.

Laid out before her eyes was the gleaming city of B'harani, a veritable jewel in the Middle East's crown. An ancient port which had grown to become one of the most developed cities in the region. Sparkling skyscrapers soaring against the mauve sky managed not to look incongruous alongside the more ancient buildings. They looked triumphant, a shining example of ambition and success.

She'd made trips here when she was a child, and while her father might have been a guest of the Sultan she and her siblings had stayed outside the castle grounds.

Samia had always loved B'harani. It had been so much more developed than Burquat had been back then. So inspirational. And nothing had changed. It had only become even more beautiful and fantastic since then. She knew that Sadiq was a keen amateur architect and had a big hand in every building that was designed. She still loved the clean, wide boulevards with plenty of trees giving leafy shade, and the numerous liberally watered green spaces where people strolled and children played.

But her favourite place so far had been the gritty docks— the oldest part of the city. It was heaving with history, a warren of ancient markets and potent smells. Ships and boats groaning under the weight of their cargoes sailed in and out of the huge harbour all day and night. And, since she'd been last, a stunningly modern marina had come to sit very sympathetically within the old port, which Samia had already vowed to come back and visit when she had more time.

She had been invisible as she'd walked around in casual trousers and a loose top, with a headscarf hiding her distinctive hair, not wanting to draw any attention in case someone had seen the tabloids in the UK. Even though she knew well that after this week she'd become one of the most recognisable faces in the country. She would be Queen to these people. As she looked out over the sprawling city now she was daunted and scared, yes, but also for the first time a fledgling sense of something else took root. It was a sense of responsibility. Ever since she'd said yes to Sadiq, the prospect of taking on such a huge role had become less about fear and more about a burgeoning sense of excitement, which alternately scared her and made her want to see what she could start doing *now*. Something she'd never have guessed she'd feel in a million years.

Her hands gripped the wall when she imagined what the reality of marriage to Sadiq would be like. What it would be like to share a bedroom, and a *bed*. Heat flowed within her lower body and she grimaced. Perhaps he wouldn't expect to share a room at all. Perhaps they would keep separate rooms and he would come to her, do his matrimonial duty and then leave.

An ominous lurching in her chest when she thought of that was so strong that she gripped the wall even tighter. She absolutely refused to investigate that surge of sudden emotion. For someone who had always vowed not to fall in love after seeing it wreak nothing but destruction she should be ecstatic at the possibility that Sadiq might want to keep things as impersonal as possible.

All she had to do was think of the perfume her maid Alia had brought her in a distinctive Al-Omari gold-and-red box. Al-Omar was famed for its perfume production all over the world, and some bottles sold for thousands of dollars. Alia had informed her that it was a gift from the Sultan, made especially to celebrate their engagement.

But when Samia had taken a sniff she'd nearly been knocked out. It was so strong. It was way too musky and overbearing for her. Nothing like the kind of delicate scent she would favour. And it had seemed to epitomise everything about her situation and the Sultan's clear lack of interest now that his convenient wife had arrived.

Sadiq let his breath out and it was unsteady—as unsteady as the pounding of his heart. Ambition and the danger of the desert, or a challenging sailing race got his heart pounding. *Not* the sight of his wife-to-be. He had been standing on the balcony terrace just outside his office when he'd seen a movement out of the corner of his eye and looked down to see Samia standing by the wall surrounding her own private terrace. She was in profile to him but he could make out the intensity of the expression on her face.

Day was tipping slowly into night—usually his favourite time to look out over the busily winding down city. But that suddenly paled into insignificance next to the sheen of light gold from Samia's hair which flowed long and wavy down to the middle of her gently arched back.

He drank in the sight of her, slender in capri pants and a figure hugging cardigan, her breasts in provocative profile, and his whole body tightened in an instant. The slow burn of desire became faster, licking through his veins as he watched her like a voyeur. A curious dismay gripped him at this rampant response. At least he could say he now desired his fiancée. But he just couldn't fathom this attraction, which only seemed to grow stronger with each passing day.

Perhaps the real root of his ambiguous feelings was the fact that she evoked something within him that no other woman ever had. Something that was fiercely primal and at the same time protective. Not even Analia had evoked such a strong mix of reactions. His mouth twisted bitterly. No. That had been much more straightforward. She'd cruelly stepped on his heart and that would never happen again.

As the day of Samia's arrival had grown nearer and nearer Sadiq had grown more irritable, not liking the sense of anticipation one bit. It was his fear of the strength of that anticipation that had led him to be so brusque when he'd welcomed her. And he hadn't liked the feeling of spreading relief at seeing her here one little bit. When he'd said he was busy he hadn't lied, but he knew he was also using it as a convenient excuse. And for someone who'd never had to make excuses in his life it wasn't a comfortable feeling.

The day he'd said goodbye to her in London, after that kiss, when she'd turned that regal profile on him and been so cool, he'd wanted to reach in and pluck her from the back of the car, carry her to his private jet and bring her straight to Al-Omar. He'd felt like one of the nomads in the desert—raw and uncultivated.

The impulse had been so strong, but he'd told himself it was just because he didn't trust that she wouldn't get cold feet. And, telling himself it was for that reason each day in the interim, he'd instructed one of his PAs to call her bodyguards and track her movements, becoming increasingly obsessed with what she was doing.

One night she'd gone to a small dinner party thrown by her work colleagues in a restaurant in Mayfair, dressed in one of her new dresses. Sadiq knew because he'd asked the bodyguard to send him pictures. It had been a perfectly modest dress—black V-neck with sleeves, and to the knee—but she'd worn her hair down and the curves she'd been hiding for years had been on display. For the first time in his life Sadiq had felt *jealous*. He'd precipitated that change and resented that other people were seeing it.

Suddenly the figure down below spun away from the wall and hurried back inside, and Sadiq realised his hands were gripping the iron railing. He consciously relaxed and looked out over the city again. His wife-to-be was proving to be a monumental distraction—something that wasn't meant to happen. The sooner he got control of himself the better. This marriage signified the next phase in development for his country. Nothing more and nothing less.

All he had to do was stop his mind straying with irritating predictability to his fiancée…

* * *

The next day Sadiq was looking out of his main study window, and he cursed colourfully enough to have his chief aide go red in the face. But he was unaware of that as he took in the scene down below in the main courtyard of his extensive stables. 'What *is* she doing?' he muttered out loud.

And then, before Kamil, his aide, could intervene, Sadiq spun around and clipped out, 'This meeting is over. Get my horse saddled immediately.' And he left the room, ignoring the open-mouthed older man, to change into something more suitable.

Belatedly Kamil rushed after him. 'But, sire, you have to meet with the committee in two hours!'

'I'll be back by then,' Sadiq said grimly, and disappeared.

Samia felt mildly guilty that she'd convinced the young groom to let her take a horse out without checking with Sadiq first. But the last thing she'd wanted to do was disturb him with such a small thing. She'd decided stoutly that as he didn't want to spend time with her, that suited her fine too. And she'd been feeling increasingly claustrophobic. Even though the Hussein castle was as stunning as it was vast, with hundreds of secluded gardens and tantalising labyrinthine corridors which would take weeks to explore, its walls seemed to be closing in on Samia. Everywhere she went someone popped out to see if she needed anything.

While she appreciated their dedication, and knew they were only doing their jobs, she craved some freedom and some space, knowing very well that once she was married her sense of claustrophobia would only increase. Her every move would be accounted for and long days of back-to-back appointments would become the norm.

When she'd seen the stables a few days ago a rare excitement had kicked in her belly. She'd used to love riding when she'd been smaller, until her stepmother had seen that joy and with typical malice had announced that it was too un-ladylike and forbidden Samia from riding again.

Unbeknownst to her stepmother, Kaden had taken Samia out on covert riding excursions, so her skills were not too rusty. The powerful stallion moved restlessly beneath her, and Samia felt the power move through those huge muscles. A sense of burgeoning exhilaration flowed through her blood. From here the gates opened straight out onto castle-owned desert lands, which led in turn to the desert proper, which then stretched for many miles to the north and away from B'harani. All the way up to Burquat, in fact. When Samia realised that she felt a pang of homesickness. Spurring the horse on, she left the castle behind and they surged forward.

Sadiq saw them in the distance, where clouds of sand were being kicked up by the powerful horse's hooves. Samia looked tiny on the back of the huge black animal, her hair streaming out behind her. She wasn't even wearing a hat, and Sadiq's blood thundered in his veins as he started to close the distance between them. He could recognise that she was an excellent horsewoman but even that didn't douse his anger.

Samia only sensed another's presence when she heard a thundering sound behind her. She looked around and saw an almost mythically huge stallion bearing down on her and the livid features of Sadiq. The realisation that it was *him* behind her, chasing her, made her turn back and speed up. She knew she was reacting to something deep and primal. A fear of this man and his effect on her, how he made her feel.

But before she knew it Sadiq had pulled alongside and had reached for her reins to bring both horses to a stop. Within the space of what felt like seconds the horses had stopped and Sadiq had jumped down and plucked Samia out from her saddle. Her legs nearly gave way, they were shaking so much, and it was only his big hands on her waist that kept her standing. He was glaring down at her and looked wild and gorgeous. A long robe was moulded to his body by the desert breeze and he'd ripped away the material of the turban that had shielded his mouth from the sand. Blue eyes like chips of diamond ice stood out in stark relief. He could have been a desert nomad. A hot beat of desire went through Samia's body.

Sudden anger at that response and at his heavy-handed behaviour rose up. She ripped herself out of his hands, praying her legs wouldn't give way. 'What on earth are you doing? You could have killed us both with a stunt like that. I would have stopped.'

He was impossibly grim. 'So why did you speed up when you saw me? You little fool. Who said you could take out one of the most dangerous horses in the stables?'

Samia was still clinging on to the reins. She recalled the pleading of the young groom for her to wait for the head groom to come back before she chose a horse, but she'd blithely assured him that she would be well able for any horse.

Guilt struck her, making her defensive. 'I'm a good rider.'

Sadiq seemed to grunt something in response. 'Galloping into the desert on a powerful horse takes skill. What would you have done if he hadn't wanted to stop? You don't know this land, and you certainly don't know that this part of the desert ends on a cliff-edge about half a mile from here and drops into a deep canyon. That's why it's undeveloped.'

Samia blanched. She hadn't known that. The thought of galloping full speed towards a cliff edge was terrifying. Terrifying enough to compel Sadiq to come after her himself. No wonder he was livid. 'I had no idea it could be dangerous.'

Despite the danger that she hadn't known about, in that moment Samia feared that perhaps Sadiq was going to be exactly like her stepmother, curtailing every bit of pleasure in her life and diminishing her until she faded away again. With that came the revelatory realisation of just how much she'd changed in the past few weeks, and it shook her to her core.

A part of herself was being reawakened—a part that had been denied for a long time—and she was scared it would be taken away from her again. The reins dropped from her hands as she gesticulated. 'Look, I'm sorry for rushing out so recklessly, but I won't be kept in the castle like some bird in a cage.' With an air of desperation tingeing her voice she said, 'You can't stop me from doing what I want.'

Sadiq looked down at the woman in front of him. The adrenalin was finally diminishing and being replaced by something hot and far more dangerous. Samia's hair was loosely tied back and fell over one shoulder in a long wavy coil of russet-gold. A silk shirt was coming loose from where it had been tucked into tight jodphurs, which were in turn tucked into knee-high leather boots.

The silk shirt was damp with her perspiration and clung to breasts which rose and fell enticingly with her unsteady breaths. He was close enough to smell her delicate scent and had a sudden memory of the box of perfume he'd approved for her as a gift. He knew instantly that it had been entirely wrong. It was more suited to the kind of woman he'd known *before*.

Giving in to the twisted inarticulate desires this woman roused inside him, he said throatily as he reached for her, 'I have no intention of stopping you doing anything once you're safe. But I *can* stop you driving me crazy.'

'What do you—?' Samia didn't get anything else out in time. Sadiq had pulled her into his tall hard body with both hands and everything was blocked out as his head descended and his mouth unerringly found hers.

The desert was gone, the horses were gone, reality was gone, and in their place was red-hot desire and a need to fuse herself to this man, to lose herself in him and block out all concerns. It was immediate and all-consuming, as if there had been some build-up within her that she hadn't even been aware of. She realised that ever since that kiss in London she'd been craving to touch him again.

She clung to the material of Sadiq's robe, registering the muscles of his chest against the back of her hands. This kiss blew their first kiss out of the water. Sadiq's tongue caressed the seam of her lips and she opened to him with a deep groan of need, clasping him even tighter when his tongue delved in and met hers, stroking along it with the sure mastery of a man who knew how to kiss, and *well*.

He clasped the back of her head, holding her captive to his erotic attack, and his other hand moved down over the curve of her waist and to her bottom, pulling her up and into him. When she felt the thrillingly hard ridge of his arousal against her soft belly Samia went still. Their breath mingled. And then an even greater sense of urgency drove her and she arched herself into Sadiq as much as she could, the hot, spiralling need within her making her feel desperate. Her breasts were crushed to his chest and her arms had risen to wind around his neck. And their kiss went on and on, getting so hot that Samia almost expected to feel flames licking up her back.

After a long moment something indefinable shifted between them and Sadiq started to pull back. Without even intending it, she gave a little mewl of protest. He pulled his head back and with excruciating slowness sanity returned to Samia's brain, along with much needed oxygen.

It seemed to take an age for her to be able to open her

eyes, and when she did all she could see were two stormy blue oceans. Her arms were around his neck, one of his hands was on her head, his other hand was cupping her bottom. His erection hadn't subsided one bit, and she had to fight not to give in to the urge to rock against him with her pelvis—a completely instinctive move, seeking friction.

Along with the shock filtering into her brain was something much more nebulous and disbelieving. He'd kissed her. Why had he kissed her? He'd kissed her as if he were a drowning man in the desert who'd just found water. Or had that been her? She'd certainly been drowning.

Instantly aware of how she was clinging to him like some kind of octopus, Samia pulled back, dislodging his hands. She felt the absurd urge to apologise, her eyes darting away from that gaze which saw too much. She felt over-hot and dishevelled. *Had* she thrown herself at him? Overcome with a build-up of desire she hadn't even acknowledged?

A hand come to her chin, forcing her to look up at him again. She was undone and he looked…amazing. Her belly clenched hard with another spurt of desire.

His mouth quirked and her belly flip-flopped. 'I can see you doubting what just happened.'

Samia went pink. Was she so easy to read?

Sadiq smiled. 'I kissed you because I've thought about little else since we last kissed. I kissed you because I wanted to kiss you—because your face, your eyes—' his eyes dropped to her mouth '—your mouth is all I can think about.'

Samia gulped, wondering if she was dreaming. She could see the horses standing restlessly just feet away. She could feel the heat of the unrelenting sun on her head. She frowned, trying to make sense of this development and the burgeoning lick of excitement within her.

'But why…why haven't you wanted to spend any time with me?'

Sadiq grimaced and let go of her chin. 'Because of exactly what just happened. I'm not in control around you...'

He cursed and spun away for a moment and Samia blinked. Not in control around her? That was as fantastical a thing for her to hear as if Sadiq had just told her they were expecting a snow shower any moment.

Obeying some urge to clarify this, or to see if he was mocking her, Samia reached out to touch his arm. He turned around and she dropped her hand, the feel of those muscles through the thin material of his robe far too disconcerting to her very shaky equilibrium.

She steeled herself. 'I don't know... What you're saying is crazy.' Sanity came back, and along with it the insecurity she'd battled all her life. He had to be lying, or jesting, or something. 'I don't believe you.'

The most powerful, gorgeous man in the world could not be standing here telling *her* that she turned him on to the point of distraction.

He looked grim. 'I couldn't believe it either.'

Samia flushed. If anything, that statement convinced her. Of course he hadn't believed this. The bookish, boring wife he'd chosen was turning into something of an anomaly. No wonder he was grim.

She hitched up her chin, emotion threatening to constrict her throat. She felt as though some long-diminished part of her was being allowed to breathe again, but Sadiq clearly resented it because it didn't fit with his plans. 'It's obvious that this isn't something you expected, but as we're to be married then surely...' Her bravado crumbled. 'Surely at least it'll make things...easier?'

He quirked a brow. 'You mean in the bedroom?'

Samia's face flamed but she nodded. Sadiq moved closer again, and Samia had trouble standing her ground.

His voice was low and wickedly seductive, all grimness

gone and replaced with sensual promise. 'It'll certainly make things more pleasurable. The only problem will be keeping my mind on issues of the state rather than my wife's delectable body. I hadn't anticipated that.'

Samia had a vivid memory of his conversation with his lawyer that first day, and how he'd laid out his reasons for wanting a conservative bride: because the stability of his country came first and he wanted no distractions. Hurt at his obvious surprise and reluctance at this turn of events had her retorting waspishly, 'I'm not going to apologise for the failure of your efforts to choose a wife so unappealing that you wouldn't have to deal with the annoying complication of attraction. Clearly it's just your libido that's rampant. I'm sure any other woman standing in front of you would be having the same effect, even one as unassuming as me.'

Samia turned and walked jerkily over to her horse, gathering the reins before finding her footing in the stirrup and swinging lithely onto the horse's back. She set off back the way she'd come, not even looking to see if Sadiq was following her. When she heard him behind her she straightened her spine and fought the urge to make a gallop for it.

Sadiq looked at the tense back of the woman in front of him. He'd almost grabbed her to him when she'd whirled away just now—to do what? he asked himself. To keep kissing her until he couldn't stop and had them both on the desert ground, making love against the unforgiving sand? Because that was what would have happened if he hadn't clawed up some elusive self-control from somewhere and stopped kissing her.

She was wrong. He couldn't imagine any other woman turning him on as she just had. Some of the most beautful women had thrown themselves at him, and one memorable time one had even been waiting naked in his bed. He'd had no problem turning his back on them.

And with the women he *had* chosen, he'd had no problem turning his back once he was done with them. He'd certainly never lost himself in a simple kiss as he just had with Samia. Something about her artless innocence mixed with that earthy sensuality made his brain turn to liquid heat.

He'd told himself that his ability to control himself with lovers had been down to the lesson harshly learnt when he'd been so young and so foolish. As if he'd consciously trained himself to control base desires. But he was realising now that the reason he hadn't lost control was because he simply hadn't felt a depth of desire so strong that it obliterated anything in its path. It was that depth of desire that made him want to ride up alongside Samia and pluck her from her saddle so that he could feel her body pressed up close to his.

Not wanting to have to think about those uncomfortable revelations, he did just that. Caution was thrown to the wind as he pulled up beside Samia. The voices in his head quietened. Reaching over, he pulled her, protesting vociferously, from the back of her horse and onto his saddle in front of him, between his legs, where his erection once again came to throbbing life. But he didn't care.

As he took the reins of her horse in one hand to lead it home he could hear her spluttering and working up to a tirade. She was tense enough to break between his legs. He bit back a smile of satisfaction and bent his head to whisper in her ear. 'Relax, Samia. And you're wrong, you know. There's not another woman on the planet right now who could induce me to lose my mind with a simple kiss.'

He snaked a proprietorial hand around her middle and felt triumphant when she relaxed against him. He could also feel when she gave up trying to articulate a reponse. He had to grit his teeth to fight the desire to move his hand down underneath those tight jodphurs to feel if his arousal pressing into her bottom was having as incendiary an effect on her as it was on him.

The rest of the ride home was as torturous as it was curiously exhilarating.

A few hours later Samia stepped out of her shower to dry off, and couldn't stop remembering how Sadiq's arousal had felt against her bottom. By the time they'd got back to the castle she'd been as weak as a kitten, all but slithering off the horse into his waiting arms.

His chief aide had been hopping up and down, babbling something about a meeting and people waiting. Sadiq had let her go after a long moment and reminded her, 'The function is tonight. I'll come for you at seven.'

And Samia had watched him walk away, disorientated and seriously bewildered by all the emotions he was arousing within her. She'd forgotten entirely about the function.

A knock came to her bathroom door then, and Samia jumped, putting her towel around her firmly before opening it to see Alia outside with a long dress on a hanger. She was dressed as all of Sadiq's servants were dressed, in impeccable white. 'I'm ready to dress you, Your Highness.'

Samia smiled at the girl, despite her sudden trepidation at the prospect of the evening ahead. 'Okay, I'll be right out.'

CHAPTER SEVEN

AN hour later Samia was waiting nervously for Sadiq. When the knock came on her door Alia opened it and stood back to let Sadiq come in, curtseying as he did so. Samia didn't notice Alia slip out, or the door close. All she saw was Sadiq in a dark tuxedo, looking almost criminally handsome, and she couldn't help but think back to that evening in the study and the singular way he'd made love to that woman. Almost as if he was looking to assuage that ennui Samia had witnessed.

He came into the room, hands in his pockets, and just looked at her for such a long, silent moment that Samia forgot about painful memories and put a nervous hand to her hair, which Alia had put in a complicated chignon. 'Alia said it was more appropriate to have it up with a dress like this.'

Sadiq quirked a small smile, making his teeth flash and heat bloom between Samia's thighs. 'You haven't looked at yourself yet?'

She flushed and shook her head, hating that he'd seen that vulnerability before.

'Come here,' he said, so softly that she almost didn't hear. But then she saw the impatience on his face and moved forward, her legs touching the silk of the dress, feeling unbearably decadent. She couldn't read Sadiq's expression, but something in it made her nerve-endings jump and sizzle. Goosebumps broke out across her skin as she stopped in front of him, and once again he took her shoulders and turned her around to face the mirror.

Reflexively Samia looked away, and heard him sigh expressively behind her. She had to get over this—so she looked back. And saw someone else standing in the mirror. For a split second she didn't actually recognise herself. The woman reflected back was a *woman*, not a girl, with her hair up and twisted into loose waves which made her neck look long and elegant.

Shadow on her eyes made them look smokily blue, the lashes long and spiky. A flush stained her cheeks and her lips looked moist and pink. Bare shoulders showed off pale skin, and when her eyes dropped they widened to see how the bodice of the silvery grey dress produced a gravity-defying cleavage.

Her eyes snapped up to Sadiq's. She brought her hands up to cover her chest. 'I had no idea—'

He smiled. 'That you had breasts?' He turned her around and kept his hands on her shoulders, burning her skin. 'Well, you do. And you look…' His gaze dropped and came back up. 'Beautiful.'

Samia opened her mouth and Sadiq put his hand over it, stopping her.

'No. I don't want to hear one word of doubt again. We will be presented to the world tonight, and you need to start believing in yourself—because if they sense even a hint of insecurity they will pounce.'

He took his hand away and Samia's mouth closed. She felt wobbly inside and all over. This whole scene was so far removed from anything she'd expected. Was he saying this just to bolster her confidence before they appeared in public? But the faint incredulity in Sadiq's tone when he'd said she was beautiful made her believe that perhaps he *had* meant it. After all, she hardly even recognised herself.

He reached into a pocket then, and pulled out a small velvet bag, opening it up to let two stunning platinum and diamond earrings fall into his hand. He handed them to Samia.

She took in a shaky breath and turned to look in the mirror to put them on. They were long and ornately elaborate, without being over the top, and swung against her neck, sparkling when she moved. She looked up at Sadiq and said huskily, 'Thank you. I'll take good care of them for the evening.'

He looked slightly bewildered by her reaction. 'They're yours, Samia. Everything I give you now is yours to keep.'

Sadiq took her hand to lead her from the room and the chaste gesture suddenly felt very intimate—because no one was there, so he didn't have to do it. *Just as he didn't have to kiss you in the desert today. But he did.*

She saw him spot the perfume bottle he'd gifted her on a table, and said hastily, while trying to block out the memory of the overpowering smell, 'Thank you for the perfume too.'

Dryly he said, 'And yet you don't wear it?'

Samia blushed behind him, cursing his powers of observation—and smell. 'I…it's lovely, but it's just a bit strong for me.'

He looked back as they reached the door, grimacing slightly. 'I realised it was all wrong for you today. I've already commissioned another scent and it should be ready for our wedding.'

'Okay,' Samia replied ineffectually as she followed him out. She was a little poleaxed at his admission that he'd realised it was wrong for her, and suddenly all those vulnerable feelings were back. She knew that if the next scent was anything close to something she'd have picked her herself she'd be in a lot of trouble.

On their walk to the main part of the castle they passed ancient stone walls with soaring ceilings, and tiny open-air courtyards where exotic peacocks stepped carefully among the plants. Burning flame lanterns lit their way, making the mosaics on some parts of the walls glint, effervescent in the light. It was truly breathtaking, and yet somehow diminished by the tall man who held Samia's hand. It was almost impossible to think of this intimidating castle as her *home*. And of this man as her husband.

Sadiq was silent until they came to the return which led to the main grand staircase leading down to the formal reception area and banquet hall. He turned and looked at her and just said, 'Ready?'

Samia was about to say, *No, and I don't think I ever will be,* but stopped herself. This was it. Her heart was beating rapidly, and jerkily she nodded her head once. 'Ready.'

Sadiq took her hand, lifted it to his mouth and kissed the inner palm, scattering Samia's brain to pieces. 'Good girl.'

And then he was leading her by the hand around the corner.

Down below there was a veritable sea of people. Women like birds of paradise in stunning gowns and glittering jewels, and men dashing in dark tuxedoes and some in more traditional robes with elaborate headdresses. Sadiq tucked her arm into his and they walked down the stairs. Samia held on tight and tried to smile, even though she felt as if she was walking into a lion-infested den.

Two hours later Samia's feet ached, her head ached and her face ached from smiling. She'd sat at Sadiq's side at dinner, and now they were mingling with the guests, who were a mix of the *crème de la crème* of Al-Omari society and visiting heads of state—like Sheikh Nadim and his wife from Merkazad.

The rest of the guests would be arriving for the wedding the following day, along with Samia's brother and sisters.

She wished Kaden could be here, but he'd been held up in London.

For a moment Sadiq was pulled away from Samia's side to speak with someone and she felt momentary panic. But just then Sadiq's mother, Yasmeena, appeared and took Samia's arm. Samia smiled. She liked the older woman.

'You look stunning tonight, my dear.'

Samia fought against her natural response to put herself down and smiled graciously. 'Thank you, Yasmeena. And you look lovely too.'

Yasmeena smiled. 'You're going to be so good for my son. I can feel it.'

Samia blushed. 'I hope I don't let him down.' And as soon as she said the words she realised that she actually meant them. Somewhere along the way her loyalties had sided firmly with Sadiq, and she felt a responsibility to him now, and to his country.

Yasmeena squeezed her arm. 'You won't. Everyone is captivated by you, Samia, you're a natural.'

Samia smiled weakly. 'I wouldn't go that far.' At that moment a movement caught Samia's eye and she looked up to see Sadiq nearby, holding court. He stood head and shoulders above everyone else, so handsome. Something inside her clenched hard.

'You like him, don't you?'

Samia's head snapped back to Yasmeena. She felt absurdly exposed. 'Well…that is, of course I like him…but it is an arranged marriage. You know that.'

She felt very defensive all of a sudden. But Yasmeena hadn't noticed. She seemed to have gone inwards to some private space, and the sadness in her amazing blue eyes was profound. She looked at Samia, smiling a little. 'I'd always hoped for more for Sadiq. I didn't want him to have the same kind of sterile marriage I had with his father. But he will be good to you. His father was…not a kind man. Sadiq is certainly not soft, but he's compassionate—which is more than his father ever was. I'm afraid we're not very close. His father guarded him jealously, and he went to boarding school so young…'

'How old was he?' Samia asked.

Yasmeena smiled sadly. 'Just eight. His father sent him to school in England—told him it would toughen him up.'

Samia's eyes were drawn back to Sadiq. He looked so composed, so sure of himself. He caught her eye and a ghost of a smile flickered across his face, making a ridiculous glow spread through her. But then his gaze fell to his mother and his smile faded. Samia shivered inwardly.

Sadiq's mother patted Samia's hand then, diverting her attention. 'You're a sensible girl. I wish I'd been so sensible at your age. I do want all the very best for you and my son.' She stopped and then started again. 'I just can't help wishing that he wasn't so cynical—'

'Mother,' came a clipped and cool voice, as a steel arm wrapped around Samia's waist, making her breath hitch, 'I need to steal my fiancée.'

Yasmeena smiled faintly, seemingly unmoved by her son's cool behaviour towards her, and then Samia was being shepherded away. She wondered why Sadiq seemed to shut his mother out, but then she was being introduced to members of Sadiq's government and she forgot about everything but surviving.

Much later Samia sent up a sigh of relief when Sadiq made excuses and led her from the room. He didn't take her hand this time as he led the way, and she tried not to be bothered, or suspect that he'd laid on the charm before the function only so that she would look suitably besotted by him. She knew that no one there would expect this marriage to be anything but an arranged match, but clearly Sadiq had his pride and wouldn't have wanted his betrothed scowling at his side.

Sadiq was waiting at the top of the stairs, and, not noticing, Samia cannoned straight into him, pitching backwards with a small cry because she had nowhere to steady herself. Quick as lightning Sadiq caught her and pulled her into his chest. Heart hammering with the sudden rush of adrenalin, Samia looked up. 'I'm sorry. I wasn't looking where I was going.'

Sadiq shook his head mock sternly. 'First you take off on a stallion, and now you're trying to throw yourself down the stairs… If I didn't know better I'd say you're still trying to get out of this marriage.'

Samia shook her head, mesmerised by the deep blue flecks in Sadiq's eyes. His arms were wrapped around her so tight that she could feel the hard strength of his chest and belly. Her breasts seemed to swell against her snug bodice.

Samia went to move back, and winced when a strand of hair caught in one of the many pins pulled sharply.

Immediately Sadiq tensed. 'Did I hurt you?'

'No.' She shook her head. 'It's just my head…my hair. It's aching.'

'Come here.' Sadiq pulled her farther along the corridor and stood her against a wall. And then he started to pull the pins out from her hair, loosening it so that it fell down around her shoulders.

Samia groaned and closed her eyes as the tension was released. 'That feels so good.'

Sadiq's voice was guttural. 'I've been wanting to do this all night.'

The last pins were out and Samia felt Sadiq's hands move through the heavy strands to her skull, where he massaged back and forth. She felt like purring. A heavy langour invaded her bloodstream and unconsciously she swayed towards him. His hands left her head and came to cup her face.

She opened heavy eyes and looked up. Her heart soared when she saw his head descend. She was ready for his kiss, mouth parted, aching to taste him again, already winding her arms around his neck and stretching up. On some level she still couldn't recognise this person she'd become, or the fact that this man appeared to find her attractive, but with each kiss it was sinking in more and more.

Sadiq gathered Samia into his arms as he drank in her sweetness. It had taken all of his restraint not to take her from that room much earlier. It had taken all of his restraint not to rip her away from perfectly banal conversations with the various men who seemed to have formed an orderly line to get to her all evening. For the first time in his life he'd been aware of only one woman in the room. *This* woman.

When he'd seen her talking with his mother he'd felt incredibly exposed. As he always did when his mother looked at him with those sad eyes.

As that realisation filtered through his consciousness Sadiq also realised that he was about to unzip Samia's dress, and that they were in one of the main corridors of the castle. He felt disorientated. But alarm bells rang loud enough to slice through the haze of desire.

Samia sensed the cool breeze of his mood-change when Sadiq pulled back. He was looking at her with something almost accusatory on his face and she quickly composed herself, hiding away her own horror at the fact that they'd been kissing like teenagers behind a bike shed. Once again she had the awful feeling that she'd thrown herself at him.

Appearing utterly in control and calm, Sadiq stood back and said, as if nothing had happened, 'I'll escort you to your room.'

Samia shook her head and tried to protest, but he was

already leading the way and Samia had to trail after him. She noticed all her hairpins spread out on the floor where where they'd been standing and went crimson. She stopped and Sadiq looked back and saw them too. A muscle jumped in his jaw when he saw Samia bend to pick them up.

'Leave them.'

She looked up. 'But—'

'I said leave them. Someone will clear them up.'

Sadiq looked so fierce for a moment that Samia quailed inside, and she straightened again, following Sadiq's tall, forbidding figure. A servant passed them and Sadiq issued a command. Samia's face burned when she thought of the state of her hair and what the servant would think when he did his master's bidding.

They reached her door and Sadiq opened it and stood back. Samia went through, childishly holding her breath as she passed Sadiq, so as not to breathe in that heady masculine scent. But it was no good, it was all around her.

'Goodnight, Samia. You did well this evening.'

She looked up at him and only saw that shuttered expression he did so well. He was a different man from the one who had been kissing her into oblivion two minutes before. She had the sensation that she was seeing tantalising glimpses of another side to Sadiq just before he clammed up again.

She smiled ruefully. 'It wasn't as excruciatingly painful as I'd expected.'

'See? I told you you'd have nothing to worry about.'

Nothing to worry about. Samia let herself be moved into yet another contortion to make it easier for the women to paint the henna tattoos on her hands and feet. It was the day before the wedding and she'd been washed, waxed and buffed from head to toe. She'd also spent an hour studying Al-Omari wedding etiquette, and Sadiq's chief aide had sat down with her to go through the exact sequence of events over the next three days. It was mind-boggling and immensely complicated.

Tomorrow would be the civil ceremony, presided over by an official. Traditionally Samia should be kept apart from Sadiq during that ceremony, as they both declared their consent to marry, but he'd told her that they would do it together, and she appreciated that nod to a more modern custom. Afterwards there would be a huge celebratory banquet.

The day after that there would be a series of appearances and lesser banquets to welcome all their guests. And the third day would be the most westernised part of the proceedings, in which she would publicly marry Sadiq in a lavish gown watched by the world's media. Followed by another sumptuous banquet and a ball.

Nothing to worry about. And yet Samia had to concede that her apprehension levels had diminished hugely since she'd weathered the function last night. She knew half of that was due in part to her preoccupation with the man she was marrying, and she shivered a little when she thought again of that kiss last night.

Hours later it was dark outside, and Sadiq was sitting at his study desk with paperwork piled high as he attempted to clear it in preparation for the wedding and honeymoon. It was impossible, though. His thoughts kept straying to one person.

Sadiq had to concede that he could see how dynamic Samia might be as Queen. He'd seen her in action last night. After she'd let go of his arm with that death grip, she'd navigated the room with an innate ease which could only have come from her background and education. More than one person had come up to him and complimented him on his choice of bride, and he hadn't been unaware of the surprise that he'd chosen someone so apparently modest and unassuming.

He'd watched how she'd put people at ease instantly with a light comment, and he'd prided himself on his initial instincts being correct. But, more than that, he'd felt *proud*. He'd also felt incredibly protective, knowing how nervous she was. But in the end she'd been quite content without him by her side, and that had left a dark emotion swirling in Sadiq's gut—to think that she didn't need him.

He sighed and pushed a hand through his hair, knowing he wouldn't get anything else done tonight. Samia had been preparing all day for the wedding, and his mind automatically visualised her naked body stepping from a steaming perfumed bath. Cursing volubly because he was thinking of her *again*, Sadiq stood up to leave the room—but his eye fell on a box on his desk. He picked it up and, telling himself that he knew exactly what he was doing, went towards Samia's rooms.

Samia was securing her dressing gown around her when she heard a knock on the door. Alia had just left, after making sure that she had everything laid out for the morning, so Samia approached the door with a smile, assuming it was her.

'Did you forget some—? Oh. It's you.'

Instantly a fine sweat seemed to break out over her skin when she saw Sadiq on the other side of the door, and she had to raise her eyeline. She felt extremely undressed in the flimsy silk night clothes.

In the same instant Sadiq silently cursed himself for coming here as he took in Samia's attire and saw how the silk moulded lovingly to the curve of her waist and breasts. He could see the dark shadow of her cleavage, the faint pink of her skin, and arousal was painfully instant. Had he really deluded himself that he would just come here and hand over what he had in his hand and then leave again?

Something within him shifted, and mentally he stepped

over a line. There was no going back now. He simply didn't have it in him to walk away from this woman.

Samia watched as some enigmatic expression crossed Sadiq's face. She felt a flutter of excitement deep in the pit of her belly.

'Can I come in?'

Samia knew she should say no and close the door in his face—for all sorts of reasons. And for all sorts of reasons she didn't. She stepped back, responding helplessly to the feral glitter in his eyes. *Lord.*

The door shut behind him and Sadiq held out a distinctive red and gold box. The new perfume. She looked from it to him and had a sudden fear of opening it. She reached out to take it, hoping he wouldn't wait for her reaction, but he lifted it high so she couldn't reach it.

Feeling utterly out of her depth, and trying to cling on to some sanity, fearing he was just toying with her, she said, 'Sadiq, what do you want? I don't think we're meant to see each other the night before the wedding.'

She was very self-conscious of the henna tattoo snaking up her hands, arms, over her feet and ankles. Sadiq's mouth curved in that slightly mocking smile she was coming to know so well.

'Those romantic notions don't apply to us.'

'Of course not.' As if she needed to be reminded. She looked down, afraid he'd see the quick dart of hurt in her chest, and then looked up again determined to make sure he was under no illusions that she harboured any such notions. 'Don't worry—I don't believe in love. I've seen how it causes bitterness and destruction.'

'Good. We're in complete agreement on that score,' Sadiq replied lightly, no expression on that harshly handsome face. 'I wanted to give you this perfume before tomorrow.'

She quashed the lancing hurt that he'd agreed so readily

with her, but she couldn't focus on that now. Her voice was far too breathless. 'So why won't you just give it to me then?'

His voice was like dark velvet. 'Because I want to show you where to place it on your body to get the most potent effect.'

'Sadiq...' she protested weakly, watching as with one hand he reached out to untie the belt around her robe. Feeling drained of all energy but the one fizzing in her blood, she half-heartedly tried to stop him. He flicked her hands away. His long fingers moving against her belly made her sway slightly, as if drunk.

With an economy of movement the belt was undone, and Sadiq gave her dressing gown a gentle pull so that it fell to the floor with a swishing sound. Now Samia was standing before him in nothing but the matching negligee, which clung like a second skin. She might as well have been naked. As she watched his eyes drift down over her body the atmosphere around them crackled with electricity. Her nipples tightened and chafed against the lace of the bodice.

Sadiq lazily took the exquisite perfume bottle out of the box and put the box on a nearby table. Without taking his eyes from hers he opened the gold top and pulled her arm towards him, placing the open end of the bottle against the hammering pulse-point of her wrist. She felt the tiniest trickle of cool liquid and could imagine it turning to steam as it hit her hot skin.

Huskily he said, 'Only a tiny amount is needed because it's so potent.'

Before the smell even hit her nostrils she just knew. This time he'd got it exactly right. It was so light it was barely discernible, and yet within seconds of mingling with her skin and pulse it became headier—a faint rose scent, winding upwards around her body. It was like the late summers she remembered in England, when the air was saturated with luxurious scents. Samia nearly closed her eyes and groaned out loud.

'I think this is more you…no?'

Samia couldn't speak. She just nodded, feeling very wobbly. Sadiq was placing some drops on the tip of his finger, and touching it to the pulse at the base of her neck, trailing that finger down over her breastbone and down farther to the cleavage between her breasts.

Samia brought up her hand to cover his and looked up at him, feeling wild with a reckless abandon and yet also not sure at all if she was ready for this. 'Sadiq, wait…we shouldn't…'

He arched that arrogant brow. 'Who says? We're our own masters, Samia. No one can tell us what to do. And I want you so badly it hurts.'

Blue eyes glittering almost feverishly, he brought the hand that covered his down and placed it over the throbbing heat of his erection. Samia looked down and saw her hand captured by his, touching him so intimately. The henna tattoo stood out like a brand, calling to her, saying, *Make this man yours.*

She lifted her gaze with an effort and it was as if nothing else outside this room mattered—only the heat between them right now. Her own voice husky, she said, 'I don't really want to stop…I want you too.'

'Good. Because I don't think I would have had the strength to turn around and walk out that door.'

The evocative scent that he'd had made for her seemed to enhance the moment, and as if in a trance Samia watched Sadiq put the bottle down on a table. He came close to her, and somehow Samia realised that they'd moved nearer to the bed. The dim lights made Sadiq's skin look golden olive. He was so beautiful he took her breath away. Completely on instinct she reached up and put her hand to his jaw, feeling the texture of his lightly stubbled skin.

She felt a muscle tense against her palm, and then Sadiq took her hand and pressed a kiss to her palm, and said with such intensity that she melted all over, *'Enough.'*

CHAPTER EIGHT

SADIQ brought her hand back down and placed it by her side. She saw him draw in a deep breath, and the thought that he had to exert control because of her made her blood sing. The thin spaghetti straps of her negligee felt incredibly flimsy as he pushed his finger under one and pulled it down her arm, and then did the same on the other side.

The thin material sank lower and lower, until it clung precariously to the fullest part of her breasts. With bated breath Samia watched Sadiq reach one finger to the valley of her cleavage to pull the material all the way down, wincing as it brushed over sensitive nipples.

She saw how the flush in his cheeks deepened, how his eyes glittered brightly. His voice was rough. 'You're so beautiful.'

For the first time Samia didn't have an immediate reflex negative reaction. But the intensity of Sadiq's expression made her come to her senses for a brief moment, and she knew she had to be honest with him before they went any further. He was reaching for her, and she stopped him by putting her hands on his. 'There's something I should tell you.'

'Yes?'

She took a breath. 'I'm not experienced.'

Sadiq smiled slightly. 'I guessed as much when we were in London.'

Samia shook her head, a little stung to think that despite her efforts to appear experienced he'd still thought her inexperienced. 'No, I mean I'm really not experienced. *At all.*'

Sadiq frowned. 'What are you saying?'

She cringed. He wasn't making this easy for her. A tinge of bitterness crept into her voice. 'I'm a virgin, Sadiq. A twenty-five-year-old virgin. Amazing as that might be to comprehend. Your analysis of my nunlike existence was accurate after all.'

Suddenly self-conscious, she pulled her nightdress back up over her breasts and turned around.

Sadiq looked at Samia's back and reeled. A virgin. How was that even possible? But all he had to do was think back to how buttoned-up she'd been when he'd first met her and he had his answer. He suspected that somewhere along the way some idiot had added to the emotional decimation carried out by the person who had made her reluctant to look at herself in mirrors.

'Who was he?' he asked now.

One of Samia's slim shoulders shrugged slightly. 'Some guy in college who'd been sent on a dare by his friends to seduce the Princess.'

Rage burnt in Sadiq's belly, and with it came a rush of something much more primal—triumphant, almost. She was his and she would be no one else's. *Ever.* He put his hands to her shoulders and turned her around, tipping her chin up so she had to look at him.

The defiantly defensive look on her face made something inordinately protective move through him. She was like a kitten, showing sharp but ineffectual claws. He twisted a long strand of silky hair around his fingers and pulled her closer. 'He was an idiot. Now...where were we?'

Sadiq had to steady his hands when he pulled the straps of her gown down again, baring those perfectly shaped breasts to his gaze. He was glad he knew she was a virgin, because he was so aroused that if he hadn't known he might have hurt her.

The way that Sadiq was so easily accepting of her innocence made her confidence bloom. Samia revelled in the way he was looking at her—as if she were the only woman in the world. She blocked out the insidious voices pointing out that every woman who'd stood before him like this must have felt the same.

That heat was building again, and with a gentle tug her nightdress fell to her waist. Sadiq reached out and cupped her breasts, testing their weight and firmness, thumbs passing over hard nipples, making them pucker even more. Samia bit her lip.

Sadiq took her hand and led her to the bed, sitting down and pulling her between his legs. With his hands holding her firm he put his mouth to one breast and then the other, making helpless sounds of pleasure come from her mouth. Her head fell back, hair tickling the base of her spine, as Sadiq sucked the peaks to stinging arousal.

She felt him pull her gown down the rest of the way until it pooled on the ground, and now all she wore was a flimsy pair of silk panties. In a move so smooth she didn't see it coming, he had Samia lying on her back on the bed, looking up at him and watching as he started to undress.

The dim light in the room highlighted his taut musculature as first his shirt came off and then his hands went to his belt. Samia sat up, her eyes drawn to the tantalising line of dark hair that led downwards underneath his trousers.

His hands stopped, and Samia heard him say, 'I want you to do it.'

Feeling gauche and nervous, Samia came up on her knees

and reached out, very aware of the henna tattoo which snaked up her arms. What she was doing felt illicit, decadent and more exciting than anything she'd ever experienced in her life.

A rush of intense longing went through her. She was all fingers and thumbs on his belt, and then the buttons and zip but then she was pushing his trousers down over lean hips, taking his underwear with them, and his impressive erection sprang free, making Samia blanch suddenly. For a moment she wasn't sure if she could do this, and doubt assailed her— the memory of baring herself before and being laughed at.

Worried, she looked up at him. 'Sadiq, I—'

He put a finger to her lips. 'Shh, don't speak.'

Sadiq kicked his clothes off and came down on the bed beside her. They lay length to length beside each other, and Samia could feel the awesome power of that arousal against her belly. Instinctively she moved, seeking friction, wanting to assuage the ache between her legs. She loved the feel of his powerful body alongside hers, all hard muscle next to her softness.

He kissed her long and luxuriously, as if they had all the time in the world. His hand drifted down over her belly to her pants. He slid it underneath and his fingers found where she was so damp and hot.

She couldn't move. She was boneless with desire as Sadiq's fingers moved in and out, alternately going faster, making her back arch off the bed towards his hand, and then slower, making her mewl with a savage frustration she'd never known before.

He pulled her panties down until she kicked them off herself. Then Sadiq pushed her legs apart until they were splayed in wanton abandonment, but Samia had gone beyond embarrassment and shame. She was this man's slave.

He slowly moved down her body, kissing his way until

he was between her legs. Samia's breath stopped altogether as with his fingers he bared her totally to his mercy, licking her with such indecent intimacy that a hectic flush rose all over her body. But that was nothing compared to the wickedly indescribable pleasure he was giving her, his mouth finding that cluster of nerves and sucking with a rhythm that was resmorseless.

'Sadiq, please…I can't…' Samia was barely coherent, her hips twitching uncontrollably as wave after wave of pleasure built and built, until Sadiq splayed a big hand on her belly, holding her down. He inserted a finger and Samia's head was almost blown off. The waves came closer together, and at a rush of pleasure almost too intense to bear Samia's entire body stilled, before falling into an ocean of exquisite aftershocks that racked every bone and cell.

Sadiq moved up over Samia's supine body. Sweat beaded his brow. It had taken more restraint than he'd thought he had not to explode before now. Especially when he'd felt the tightness of her body and the contractions of her orgasm. He'd never known a woman to be so responsive. He'd always prided himself on being a good lover, but every woman he'd been with had somehow given the impression of holding something back—as if they were too aware of themselves to let go completely. But Samia held nothing back. She was unrestrained and wild.

To think that he'd once dismissed her as plain and conservative. The thought was laughable now as he took in her luscious curves, the flush on her rosy-tipped breasts and that glorious hair spread out around her head. A light sheen of perspiration made her skin glow. Her eyes were slumberous as she looked at him. With an ominous lurch in his chest he came over her and pressed a kiss to soft lips, loving the way she opened her mouth and sought his tongue, exploring his mouth with a studied thoroughness that had him pulling back for fear of losing it completely.

Praying for control, he settled between her spread thighs and with extreme care slowly slid the engorged head of his erection along her wet folds. Samia moved her hips towards him, causing him to slip inside her a little, and he gritted his jaw.

'Wait…I have to take this…slowly. I don't want to hurt you.'

'You won't…' Samia said the words but had no idea if he would or not. All she knew was that she wanted to be joined with this man in the most basic and primitive way.

With a groan, Sadiq thrust into Samia and at first she wondered what all the fuss about hurting her was about. And then he thrust again, and a more intense pain than she'd ever felt sent shockwaves to her brain. It was blinding and white-hot.

Instinctively recoiling from Sadiq's heavy weight and that pain, she tried to pull back, while at the same time perversely not wanting to break the connection. She let out a small sound of agony she couldn't hide.

'I know…' he soothed. 'I'm sorry. It'll hurt just for a bit.'

'Sadiq…' Samia sobbed in earnest, gripping his arms. The pain was intensifying. 'I don't know if I can—'

'I know it hurts. But just trust me, okay?'

Eyes huge and watering, Samia looked up at him and nodded, biting her lip.

'You need to try and relax, *habibti*…you're so tight.'

The term of endearment struck her somewhere very vulnerable. Samia took a deep breath and concentrated on relaxing the muscles which even she could feel were like a vice around Sadiq. And when she did that she could feel the solid length of him slide a little deeper, as if something had given way. Immediately, magically, the pain started to lessen, and she breathed out slowly on a shuddery breath.

'Okay?' Every sinew seemed to be pulled taut across Sadiq's chest.

Overcome with a wave of something that felt suspiciously tender, Samia nodded and Sadiq kept going, with almost excruciating slowness, deeper and deeper, until Samia felt as if he'd touch her very heart. And then he slowly withdrew, until he was almost out completely. This time when he thrust in the tightness had eased a little more, and a tremor of pleasure skated along Samia's nerve-endings. Relief was overwhelming, and she could feel her muscles relaxing even more.

She bent her legs, and Sadiq groaned as he buried himself inside her. He pressed a kiss to her mouth as he started up a slow, gentle rhythm in and out that made those tremors of pleasure turn into something much stronger.

Soon the pain was forgotten completely as she arched upwards and closer to Sadiq, chest to chest, relishing it when he slid so deep within her that she could feel no space between them. His pace quickened, his breathing grew unsteady and Samia could see the dark blush of colour staining his cheeks, the sweat on his brow.

Instinctively wrapping her legs around him, she couldn't help a deep moan escape her lips as an incredibly pleasurable tension wound inside her. It built and built like the waves had before, only this was about ten times more intense. The feel of Sadiq's powerful body moving in and out with such relentless precision finally made the tension snap, and Samia gripped him tight with her thighs as his body ground into hers and she felt the warm release of his seed inside her.

For a long moment, as the tremors of pleasure subsided in both their bodies, all that could be heard was ragged breathing and pounding hearts. Samia's legs were wrapped tight around Sadiq, binding him to her body. She loved everything about the feel of his heavy weight, on her and in her.

Eventually Sadiq moved and Samia had to let him go, reluctantly, wincing slightly as he extricated himself. He lay on his back beside her, eyes closed. Samia felt nakedly vulnerable and looked for a cover, but his voice stopped her.

'Are you okay? Did you bleed?' He sounded curiously detached, and it sent a sharp dart to Samia's heart. She looked down blankly and saw that there was indeed some blood on the exquisite bedcover. An irrational wave of guilt washed over her, and embarrassment too. A cool wind seemed to be emanating from Sadiq and she wanted to be alone, to try and make sense of what had happened. One minute she'd been about to go to bed alone, and the next...she was no longer a virgin.

'Yes, there's some blood,' she said quietly, moving to get off the bed. 'I'll get something to clean it.'

An arm held her back. 'I'll take care of it.' His voice was gruff.

Sadiq got up and walked to the bathroom, switching on a light and effortlessly highlighting the supreme perfection of his physique. He was utterly unselfconscious as he disappeared, and then steam quickly filled up the cavernous bathroom. He'd obviously turned on the shower.

With a wince as she felt how tender she was, Samia got off the bed, picking up her discarded dressing gown. She pulled it on, tying it securely with a shaking hand, and picked up her panties and nightgown too, before hovering uncertainly. She didn't know what to do.

Sadiq emerged from the bathroom again, steam billowing out behind him and as gloriously naked as the day he was born. Feeling absurdly embarrassed, Samia said stiffly, 'Can you put some clothes on?'

She averted her eyes and heard his dry response. 'It's a bit late for that now, don't you think?'

But she sighed with relief when she heard him pull up a zipper, and sneaked a look to see him finish buttoning his shirt. He picked up what she saw was a damp towel—presumably to clean the blood—and her heart beat unevenly.

She put out a hand, mortified that he was even still here, witnessing this. 'Please, I'll do that. You should go. I'm sure it wouldn't look good to be found in my room on our wedding morning.' She attempted to sound light. 'It wasn't in the etiquette book.'

It was only when Sadiq looked at Samia that he felt as if he was finally coming back to his senses. For a long moment he'd felt a little concussed. His brain numb after the onrush of too much...pleasure.

He wanted to go and pull Samia back into his arms, carry her into the shower and wash her from head to toe himself. And then he wanted to take her back to bed and pleasure her until she couldn't move a muscle. But something in her rigid stance made him stop. He might have suspected that he'd hurt her, but he'd felt the powerful contractions of her orgasm. She would be sore, though. She'd been so tight.

This intensity of feeling...it had to be because she'd been a virgin. *Had to be.* He hadn't even used protection, and as much as he wanted heirs he certainly hadn't planned on *this*. This surge of a desire so strong that there'd been no time for a rational discussion about anything.

Feeling exposed in a way that was becoming horribly familiar with this woman, he put down the towel and said, 'You should have a shower. You'll be sore.'

Samia flushed with embarrassment and silently pleaded with Sadiq to leave so she could be alone and make sense of what happened. 'Yes...I will.'

She felt rather than heard him come close, and despite

the tenderness in her body she was already melting and responding. He tipped up her chin so she couldn't avoid his eyes and she cursed him inwardly. For a moment he didn't speak, and tension coiled deep in her belly. His eyes were stormy again, and there was some emotion that made her hold her breath. Finally his mouth quirked in a tight smile. 'I don't think I handled that very well.'

Samia blinked. She would imagine he hadn't had to say anything like that to a woman for a long time—if ever. 'What do you mean...? It was...' She blushed even harder. 'It was fine.'

It had been more than fine. Sex with Sadiq had exploded the very secret fear that she might be frigid and she'd tasted paradise. *Fine* was a ridiculously ineffectual word for what had just happened.

His jaw clenched. 'I meant afterwards... I'm not the cuddly type, Samia. And I'm sorry you bled. I hope you're not too sore. But I'm not sorry we slept together. And when we return from our honeymoon you'll be moving into my rooms.'

Samia's face was stained a delicate pink that had Sadiq almost carrying her back to the bed to take her again, even though he knew he couldn't. She had to recover. She bit her lip and looked away, before looking back with such artless sensuality that his body throbbed painfully.

'I'm not sorry we slept together either...and the pain...it wasn't so bad.'

Sadiq could remember the way her eyes had watered, beseeching him to ease that pain. He gritted his jaw to stop himself from bending down to kiss those swollen lips. He backed away while he still could, because despite what he'd just said he was suddenly feeling the urge to offer to spend the night in her bed, just *sleeping*. 'Get some sleep, Samia. You're going to need it.'

It was only when Sadiq had closed her door behind him that he realised he'd not planned on sharing his rooms with his wife at all. He'd planned on keeping his own private space, anticipating that the marriage bed would be purely a functional place. But suddenly everything had changed, and there was no way he could contemplate that Samia wouldn't share his bed for the foreseeable future. He was going to find it hard enough to get through the wedding without touching her.

He reassured himself as he walked to his own room that once his desire for her diminished they would renegotiate sleeping arrangements.

Samia looked at the henna tattoo as the hot water sluiced down her body in the shower and saw that some of it had run and become smudged. She'd have to ask Alia to get the women to refresh it in the morning, and she wondered if they'd be able to tell what had happened.

Her head and heart were all over the place. She wasn't sure how she felt any more—about anything. She thought of Sadiq's stark statement that she'd be moving into his rooms, and the prospect of repeating the intensity she'd just experienced night after night was overwhelming.

The whole anatomy of this marriage was changing almost by the minute, resembling nothing close to what she would have imagined in London. She put her hands to her belly under the spray, recalling the warm rush of his release deep inside her. Her heart clenched. His obvious lack of concern about contraception said it all. Not to mention her part in that unforgivable oversight. But in all honesty she'd thought that they'd discuss things rationally before embarking on the physical side of things. There had been nothing rational about tonight.

Her hands trembled on her belly and Samia turned and

rested her forehead against the marble wall while the water sluiced down her back. She could already be pregnant with Sadiq's baby. She knew that for him it would be a mere tick on the list of his things to do after marrying his convenient wife, but for Samia the future wasn't looking so black and white any more, and she had an awful sick feeling that all her lofty notions about love were about to be seriously challenged.

CHAPTER NINE

ON the final and last evening of the wedding celebrations Samia felt wrung out and extremely on edge. She was sitting alone for a rare moment, in the palatial banqueting hall where she and Sadiq had repeated their vows earlier in the day for the second time, in front of a huge crowd. The wedding band was heavy on her finger, glinting in her peripheral vision like a brand. She was now married to Sadiq. He was her *husband*.

He was just feet away, talking to her brother, his broad back to her, making her think of what it had been like to rake her fingernails down it to his muscular buttocks, when he'd shattered her in pieces the other night.

She sighed deeply. She wondered now if it had been a distant dream. Sadiq hadn't shared her bed again since then, and Samia would like to be able to say that she'd been relieved—but she couldn't deny that at every moment over the past three days she'd been acutely aware of Sadiq and had had to battle flashbacks to the sounds of their hearts beating in deafening unison and the way he'd felt between her legs.

It had felt wickedly decadent to know that they'd already been intimate, but that had quickly turned to frustration as Sadiq had seemed determined to keep Samia at arm's length—sometimes visibly flinching if she touched him, even in the rare moments they'd been alone. As a result she now felt incredibly sensitive and raw. Especially after seeing all the beautiful female guests one by one making a beeline for Sadiq. She'd had to wonder which of the more cloying ones had been his lovers.

Adding to her sense of dislocation and being on edge had been the fact that her brother had turned up with the last woman Samia would have ever expected to see him with again. The Englishwoman who had broken his heart years before. When Samia had raised an enquiring brow as Kaden had introduced Julia to Sadiq, he'd just quelled her with a fierce look, and she hadn't had a chance to question him since then.

The first ceremony had been the most understated—the two of them alone in a room with a handful of official witnesses who had listened to them pledge their vows. The stark language and lack of frills had made it somehow more moving and momentous in a way which she knew it shouldn't have been. After that, they'd been married. But that short ceremony had been only the start of the most colourful and frenetic seventy-two hours of Samia's life.

It all felt slightly unreal now, like a blur. She'd gone through the motions, saying her vows to Sadiq for a second time in the more grandiose western-style service earlier. She'd been relieved when it hadn't had the same effect as the first time round, afraid that some emotion would rise up unbidden and reveal something she wasn't ready to share with herself, never mind the vast ogling crowd.

For the first two days she'd been relatively demurely dressed, in a selection of traditional Al-Omari kaftans and veils that had been made in Paris, and had changed into more elaborate couture gowns for the evenings. She'd been absurdly happy and touched to see that Sadiq had asked Simone to come for the wedding. The no-nonsense Frenchwoman had been on hand to help her in and out of the umpteen changes all weekend, and had just helped her out of the ornate wedding gown and into a dark blue evening gown.

Her husband turned now, and those blue eyes seared right through her. Samia knew she was in a dangerous mood because she was feeling so sensitive and self-conscious. Three days of being under intense scrutiny was pushing her to her limit. He walked towards where she sat and a hush fell around the room. Sadiq was resplendent in the Al-Omari military uniform, a sword hanging by his side in a jewelled scabbard. He put out a hand and Samia placed hers in his palm. It was time for their first public dance. It would be their most intimate contact in days.

Trembling all over, from fatigue and something more volatile, she let him lead her to the dance floor. With distinct irritation in his voice Sadiq said near to her ear, 'If it's not too much trouble, do you think you can manage a fake smile at least? There are about five hundred spectators watching our every move. I know this is trying for you, but it's nearly over.'

They were practically the first words he'd directed at her since they'd exchanged vows earlier. Inexplicably it made tears smart at the back of Samia's eyes, because she felt as if she'd been playing the role of a lifetime, smiling and pretending that crowds of people didn't terrify her; the only thing keeping her going had been Sadiq's solid presence by her side. But with those few words Sadiq was letting her know that her innate discomfort in this milieu had been all too evident, and their intimacy of the other night felt even more like a distant dream.

Samia hated this rollercoaster of emotions she seemed to be on, and, feeling very shrewish, looked up, her long dress not diminishing the powerful feel of Sadiq's body one bit. 'And of those five hundred I'd suspect that at least three hundred are lamenting the loss of a lover.'

Sadiq's hold tightened almost painfully, and with a dangerous smile on his face he looked down and said, 'Jealous, Samia? There's actually only two hundred women here, so unless you're counting some of the men as conquests of mine also…?'

His cool arrogance made her want to spin out of his arms and leave the dance floor. Heat and tension surged between them, and then he uttered something guttural in a dialect that Samia didn't even recognise and he was kissing her. She wasn't aware of the tumultuous applause. She was only aware that she'd been waiting like a starving person for Sadiq to kiss her again properly. The chaste touches of their lips after the vows had been like a form of torture.

When he finally broke the kiss she was pliant in his arms, staring up at him, dazed. He looked impossibly grim.

'Do you really think I would be so crass as to invite ex-lovers to our wedding and put you in a position where people could talk or mock? And, while I'm flattered that you think me capable of it, the number of women who have graced my bed is far less than you seem to imagine. The only woman here that I want is standing right in front of me.'

Samia was stuck for words, feeling incredibly chastened even as an illicit bubble of joy rose upwards. Before she could make a complete ass of herself Sadiq continued dancing, as if the explosive moment hadn't just happened.

Somehow Samia got through the rest of the evening, buoyed up by Sadiq's words and the way he clamped her to his side.

Later, when he walked her to her room, Samia felt remorse clawing upwards. She knew the past few days had been trying for him too. She was also terrified he might read something into her jealousy. She turned to him outside her door and bit her lip before saying in a rush, 'I'm sorry…about earlier. I don't know what got into me. I'm just…a bit tired.'

Sadiq's jaw was tense. And then he sighed deeply, raking a hand through his hair. 'I'm sorry too. I didn't mean to be critical. I know how hard it must have been to have everyone staring at you like an exhibit in a zoo. And you've been amazing.'

Samia immediately felt a warm glow infusing her whole being. Shyly she said, 'Really?'

Sadiq looked tense again. 'Yes. Really.'

For a moment Samia thought he was about to kiss her, but then he stepped back and said, 'Tomorrow morning, early, we leave for Nazirat. Be ready.'

Sadiq stood outside Samia's closed bedroom door for a long moment while the waves of desire pounded through his body, not abating one bit. He'd never wanted a woman so badly. A mixture of ambiguous feelings made him wary, though. The past three days had not been the tedious ritual he might have expected. As he'd been saying his vows at that first ceremony, looking at Samia's veiled and downbent head, a completely unexpected wave of emotion had surged up. He'd put it down to gratitude that he'd found the right bride for him.

And she had been…amazing. Cool, calm, dignified. The perfect bride. More than he could have hoped for. Every atom of her being exuded her lineage and background with effortless grace. He wouldn't have believed the transformation if he hadn't seen it with his own eyes, but she was no longer the awkward woman he'd first met. It hadn't stopped him feeling inordinately protective, though, because he'd sensed it was a brittle shell hiding her insecurity.

The only time she'd shown a hint of strain had been this evening, and he cursed himself now for being so harsh on her. But when he'd seen her pale, unsmiling face, he'd thought back to how reluctant she'd been to marry him. Guilt had surged upwards. And that had brought too many unwelcome reminders of his own parents' marriage. His mother's reluctance and his father's vitriolic rage.

Sadiq kept assuring himself this was different—because he wasn't obsessed with Samia the way his father had been obsessed with his mother. And yet with an uncomfortable prickling feeling Sadiq knew that the passion he felt for Samia was close to bordering on the obsessive. He assured himself again: he respected Samia and they both knew where they stood. This *was* different.

He thought of her comment earlier on the dance floor; she'd been *jealous.* Normally when a woman exhibited that emotion it made him run fast in the opposite direction. But with Samia…it had enflamed him. Turned him on. And he'd kissed her in front of that crowd of relative strangers like a starving man falling on a feast.

He finally backed away from the door and smiled grimly when he thought of the honeymoon ahead. One week with Samia alone in an oasis paradise in the desert. One week to get this fixation out of his system so that when they returned to B'harani his desire would not be this all-consuming need and he would be able to get on with his job.

Samia realised that Sadiq hadn't been joking when Alia woke her at five the following morning. She was hustled out of bed, dressed, and was blinking in the dawn light outside when Sadiq pulled up in a Jeep, looking dark and gorgeous in jeans and a casual jumper. Instantly Samia was awake and on high alert.

Sadiq barely looked at her though, brusque to the point of rudeness, and they drove to a small landing pad where a helicopter was waiting.

After a thirty-minute journey over the undulating landscape of the desert that changed colour as the sun rose, they landed near a modest-sized castle. Sadiq took her arm in a firm grip.

Samia figured that the only possible reason for his bad mood had to be because he was dreading the idea of spending a week in the desert, alone with her. Familiar insecurity constricted her insides. How could it be anything else? She was so inexperienced; he was highly sexed. The other night had to have been a disappointment for him.

She cursed herself again for having shown that she was jealous. She'd let fatigue and tension get to her, and she couldn't let that happen again.

But as soon as they were alone in a huge and stunning bedroom which seemed to open out directly onto the vast desert he turned to her with ferocity in his eyes.

'Come here,' he ordered in a rough voice, and Samia moved to him as if in a dream, half scared at the look on his face and half thrilled.

As soon as she was close enough he pulled her to him and his eyes roved over her face as if he'd never seen her before. His hand was busy undoing her hair so that it fell in thick waves down her back.

'That's better. I was afraid to speak on the way here in case I started kissing you and couldn't stop. The last three days have been the longest days of my life.' He tipped up her chin. 'Do you have any idea how hard it's been to watch you parading around in those stunning dresses and not pull you behind a column so that I could strip you bare and make love to you until you were screaming my name and I couldn't remember who I was?'

Heat flooded Samia and confusion reigned, along with an awful burst of hope within her breast. 'But…last night you didn't…?' She bit her lip for a second and blurted out, 'I wanted you to make love to me. But I didn't want to…ask.'

Sadiq smiled, and it looked slightly pained. 'I don't know

how I walked away from you but I wanted to make sure you were fully recovered. Because I don't intend to let you out of bed for this whole week. Starting now...'

And he took her face in his hands and kissed her until she was boneless. When he picked Samia up and carried her to the bed she was trembling all over with the anticipation and build-up of the last three days.

Later, with no idea how much time had passed, Samia woke but kept her eyes closed. She was naked, face-down in a soft bed, and she'd never felt so completely and utterly—

'Good evening, *habibti*...how are you feeling?'

Samia smiled. She couldn't keep it in. But she didn't open her eyes for fear of making this dream end. Her voice sounded indecently husky. 'I feel like I won't be able to move ever again.'

A dark, sexy chuckle was accompanied by a hot kiss on her bare shoulder, and then the bed dipped and Sadiq got out. Reluctantly Samia opened her eyes and watched the impressive back view of her naked husband as he walked across the luxurious room to the *en suite* bathroom. Whatever she'd experienced that first night in Sadiq's bed had been surpassed, and she knew with a little shiver of pleasure that it was only going to get better. Never in her wildest dreams or fantasies had she imagined that sex could be so...amazing.

Samia turned onto her back and looked out to see dusk falling over the dunes in the distance through the open doorway. They'd been in bed all day. And they were utterly alone, utterly remote. No one but them and the discreet staff and some of Sadiq's security men in another lodging nearby. They were deep in the desert interior of Al-Omar, majestic in its isolation. The closest civilisation was the oasis town of Nazirat, some twenty miles away.

This ancient fortress castle had been built on a small

neighbouring oasis some three hundred years previously, but Sadiq had made improvements along the way and now it was a luxurious hideaway. Alia had told Samia that apparently one of his ancestors had built it for a favoured wife. The romanticism struck a dangerous chord in Samia.

Through the open doors she could also see the still water of their private pool, the low divans around it piled high with opulent cushions and throws. Candles flickered softly in tall glass lanterns. The gentle breeze was warm. A feeling that she'd never experienced before stole over her. Samia frowned, trying to pinpoint what it was, and with a flash realised that it was contentment. And peace.

She wondered for a moment if she was in fact dreaming, because she'd never been given to dreamy introspection before, but the tenderness between her legs told her otherwise. Just then Sadiq emerged naked from the bathroom, walking towards the bed with singular intent and a wicked gleam in his eyes. If this was a dream Samia knew she didn't want to wake up just yet.

Before she could draw breath he'd plucked her up off the bed into his arms and was striding back towards the bathroom. The steam of the huge shower enveloped them like a luxurious warm mist. Within minutes of stepping under the powerful spray Sadiq was soaping her body with a thoroughness that had a visible effect on him, and Samia was all but begging him to take her, right there.

She'd obviously spoken aloud, because he tipped her head back, cocooning her from the spray with his big body. 'Believe me, I want to, *habiba*, but you're still tender. And we need to use protection. But don't worry…I won't always be so considerate.'

It was only then that Samia realised that Sadiq *had* been careful and used protection. But before she could ask him about it Sadiq was turning her around and rinsing off her back. She felt him go still behind her.

Sounding completely shocked, he said, 'You have a tattoo.'

She'd forgotten all about the tattoo across her lower back, just above her buttocks. Something rebellious rose up within her at his shocked tone and she turned around. 'Yes, I have a tattoo. Is that so hard to believe?'

Sadiq looked at her and she found the indignant look on his face slightly funny. She could well imagine that when he'd been vetting her for her suitability he wouldn't in a million years have dreamt she'd have a tattoo.

'Where did you get it done?'

'In New York with my friends, before we sailed across the Atlantic. We all got different ones which meant something personal to us.'

Sadiq switched off the shower with an abrupt move and grabbed a towel, wrapping it around Samia.

'What is it?' she asked, more hesitantly than she would have liked. 'Are you really so shocked?'

Sadiq tried to school his features as he busied himself rubbing Samia dry, which of course was entirely too distracting in itself. It was ridiculous, but in some way he felt slightly betrayed...*by a tattoo.* Samia was looking at him expectantly, her skin soft and glowing and more seductive than she could ever know.

He forced himself to be rational and quirked a wry smile. 'A tattoo is not something I associated with the mouse who came into my study that first day in London.'

Samia flushed pinker and looked away, and perversely that made Sadiq feel comforted. He caught her chin and brought her head up so he could inspect those blue depths. Curbing his insatiable desire to rip the towel away and do what she'd just been begging him to do in the shower, he asked gruffly, 'What does it mean?'

'It's the Chinese symbol for strength.'

Sadiq saw something intensely vulnerable flash in those aqaumarine depths and had to drive down a spark of emotion. It made his voice more curt than he would have intended. 'Let's have dinner and you can tell me all about why you'd want a symbol for strength tattooed onto your skin.'

He watched Samia walk into the bedroom and dither for a moment before self-consciously pulling on the kaftan which had been left out for her, leaving the towel around her till the last minute. Clearly she was not used to this kind of intimacy, and evidently Sadiq had become too jaded from seeing lovers eager to display their naked bodies to him, because watching Samia was like watching the most erotic striptease he'd ever seen.

He saw the tattoo again just before it was covered up by the kaftan dropping over her body and had to admit it was sexy, positioned where it was just above the jut of her buttocks, where only someone intimately acquainted with her body would see it.

As he dressed himself and tried to control his insatiable libido, which was responding helplessly to that image, he had to admit to a slight feeling of disorientation. Samia was turning into something of an enigma, and this was something Sadiq had not accounted for. Nor he was even sure he particularly welcomed it.

An hour later they were sitting on an open-air terrace on the level below their bedroom. A table for two had been set with flickering candles. Chilled white wine was in beautiful goblet-style glasses. The discreet staff, dressed in the same white clothes that were a trademark of the Hussein castle, had been flitting to and fro, serving a range of delicious delicacies for them to feast on.

Samia loved the rustic nature of the dinner—the fact that the table was bare and plain, despite obviously being an antique and inlaid with mother of pearl mosaics. The feel of the raw silk of the kaftan against her skin was like an erotic caress, and she had to stop herself squirming in her seat, already wantonly wishing they were back upstairs in that huge bed with nothing between them. She was also desperately hoping that Sadiq wouldn't remember what he'd said.

But, in that uncanny way he had of honing in on her most private thoughts, he sat back, took his wine glass in his hand and looked at her. 'So...tell me. Strength. What did you need strength for?'

Samia wiped her mouth with her napkin and looked across the table at Sadiq. She'd been avoiding looking at him because in this flickering light, with a hint of stubble on his jaw, he looked so gorgeous... She sighed. He was waiting for her answer.

Why did it have to be Sadiq who wanted to hone in on the workings of her psyche? She looked down and pleated her napkin nervously. 'I told you before about my stepmother?'

He nodded. 'You said you didn't get on?'

Samia nodded and looked up, took a sip of wine for fortitude. 'I got the symbol for strength because embarking on that sailing trip I felt as if I was strong—for the first time in my life. After years of feeling weak.'

She flashed a brittle smile at Sadiq, hating how vulnerable this was making her feel.

'Alesha despised me from the moment she saw me, for all sorts of reasons, but mainly because I looked like my mother. It was common knowledge that my father and mother had shared a great love. He visited her shrine every day religiously until he died.'

She grimaced slightly. 'Alesha used to tell me from when I was tiny that because I looked like my mother it made it harder for my father to be around me, because I was the reason she died.'

'Samia—'

She cut him off, pretending not to hear him, not wanting him to think she was looking for sympathy. 'Her forte was targeting people's weak spots. She used it to chip away at my self-confidence, constantly pointing out how different I was. Things got worse when she had girl after girl and no precious male heir to counteract Kaden's supremacy and mine.'

Samia's voice had become a monotone, as if she could try and hide the emotion she felt. 'If I found anything I enjoyed doing, she'd stop me. It was a constant war of attrition and I couldn't fight her.'

Sadiq said dryly, but with a steel tone, 'She sounds utterly charming.'

Samia looked at him and was relieved not to see pity. Her heart pounded a little at the look in his eyes. 'She was, you see—to anyone on the outside looking in. She was an arch manipulator, angry and bitter because she knew my father didn't love her. I was meant to give a piano recital one day in our huge banquet hall, for my father and some important guests—' Samia stopped. What was she doing, babbling on about mundane childhood incidents?

But Sadiq inclined his head. 'Go on, Samia. I want to hear this.'

Cursing herself for bringing this up, she continued reluctantly, 'I'd practised for weeks on my mother's piano. She'd nearly become a concert pianist before she met my father, and when I played I felt somehow…close to her. Not that I had half her talent.' She blushed, feeling silly, but Sadiq was still looking at her with something unfathomable yet encouraging in his eyes.

Samia took a deep breath. 'Alesha took me aside just before I went on. I don't even remember what she said now, but when I sat down...I froze. I couldn't remember a note of the music and I couldn't move. All I can remember is excruciating terror, not knowing how to just get up and leave. Kaden had to come and physically lift me off the stool. I'd let my father down in front of his guests—but, worse than that, I felt I'd let my mother's memory down. I haven't touched a piano since.'

She grimaced at herself now. 'It's all so mundane really. My childhood was no worse than many others. Alesha was just a bully. Apart from her we had a perfectly stable and secure background.'

Almost harshly, Sadiq cut in. 'No, it's not. Nothing is mundane, when you're a child and your world is threatened. You can have the most secure background and yet within that lies any number of threats.'

Samia looked at him, her eyes growing wide. 'Why do you say that?'

His jaw clenched. 'Because it's true. My world was threatened every day when my father took his anger at my mother out on me—or her. Whoever was closest. I watched my father kick her so hard in the belly once that she lay there bleeding. But he wouldn't let me help her. I tried to, but he beat me back.'

Samia sucked in a horrified gasp. 'How could he have done such a thing? And let you watch?'

Sadiq smiled grimly. 'So that I would know how to deal with a disobedient wife. A wife who wouldn't give him any more children.'

Samia shook her head, feeling sick. 'You would never be capable of such a thing. How old were you?'

Sadiq shrugged now. He felt curiously raw at Samia's easy assertion that he was not like his father. 'About five.'

Samia shook her head. 'Sadiq, that's horrific. Is that why she didn't have any more children?'

'She didn't have any more children because my father slept with mistresses while she was pregnant with me and then passed on a sexually transmitted disease to her. She wouldn't sleep with him after that, and as a result of his pride and refusal to seek treatment he became infertile.'

The disgust he felt whenever he thought of his father was rising inside Sadiq, and he wondered wildly for a moment how on earth they'd strayed onto a subject he never discussed with anyone.

'Is that why you doubted your own fertility? Or why you can't look at your mother? Because you feel guilty that you weren't able to protect her?'

Samia's question hit Sadiq right in his gut. He saw Samia's huge, expressive eyes shimmering suspiciously and put down his napkin. 'I think we've had enough conversation for one evening.'

Samia watched Sadiq stand up to his full impressive height. Her heart ached in a very peculiar and disturbing way. He looked so remote and proud. He was obviously angry with himself for having revealed what he had, and she'd gone too far with that question.

But she'd been no less forthcoming—as if someone had injected her with some kind of truth serum. She could have made up any old cliché about why she'd got the tattoo. She wasn't meant to be feeling anything for this man. When he put his hand out now she took it gratefully, suddenly as eager as he was to change the subject.

Afterwards, when Samia's head was on Sadiq's chest with his strong heartbeat under her cheek, she thought of something and said, 'You're using protection now...'

She lifted her head and looked at him, and a wave of

shyness washed over her to think that he'd just made love to her and had done so with such passion that she was still floating in a limbo of languorous satedness. Sadness gripped her at the thought that this would not last. It couldn't. If he wasn't already growing bored with her limited range of responses, he would be very soon. And she hated the self-pity that that thought engendered.

He'd gone very still for a moment, and then he looked at her, and those eyes were unreadable and his jaw was tense. He moved then, and manoeuvred them so that Samia was on her back and he was on one elbow, looking down at her.

Her insides contracted. Lord, but he was gorgeous. It was almost intimidating. The languorous bliss in her body was dissipating slightly under the cool look in his eyes.

'I thought that it would be a good idea to give ourselves some time to get to know one another before getting pregnant.'

'Oh…' Samia said ineffectually. So that was the reason for his suddenly using protection.

Sadiq twitched back the sheet from where it covered Samia's body and she flushed under his blatant appraisal. 'But as you could already be pregnant, and part of the requirements of this marriage are heirs, I don't see the advantage any more.'

And before she could speak, or formulate a response to that, Sadiq had drawn her up over his body, legs either side of his hips, where she could feel the potent strength of him against her moist core.

Samia had the feeling he was angry about something and taking it out on her, but she was too distracted by the feel of his erection. The sensation of hot skin to hot skin was too much. With a small groan of helpless desire she slid down onto his hard length and forgot all about anything but this delicious insanity.

* * *

Sadiq couldn't sleep, and he wasn't surprised. He'd just acted like a complete neanderthal and taken his own self-anger out on Samia in a very cavalier fashion. Not that she'd complained. He'd never slept with any woman so impassioned, so responsive and so giving. His heart thumped ominously. He came up on one elbow and looked at her, skin still flushed with their lovemaking, lashes long against her cheek.

He could still see her sitting astride him, and the look of pure shocked bliss on her face as she'd realised that she could dictate the pace of their lovemaking—much to his intense torture, her evident delight and an eventual climax that had been so strong he'd blacked out for a split second. A first for him.

With a muted groan he got out of the bed and pulled on his robe, crossing to the ornately trellised wall which surrounded their private terrace. The desert lay spread out before him. *Dammit.* He brought his clenched fist down on the wall. He *had* intended talking to Samia about birth control. He *had* thought it would be a good idea to wait at least for a few months, to let her get used to life at the castle.

He was uncomfortably aware that his decision had come *after* that first night. *After* he had been driven by blind aching need and any rational thought of anything other than sating the fire in his body had precluded a sane discussion about birth control. It had only been in the sober moments during the wedding that he'd realized what a risk he'd taken.

When she'd asked the question just now, she'd reminded Sadiq uncomfortably of his own woeful neglecting to be responsible. Guilt had struck hard, and all he'd been able to think of was everything he'd just told her, which he'd never shared with another person. She'd shared something with him so had he felt obliged to spill his guts too? Once again he'd reacted from a visceral place to the threat she was posing to his once very equable life. A life he'd naively thought wouldn't suffer so much as a ripple due to his marriage.

He wasn't facing a ripple now. It was a storm of unprecedented power on the horizon. This marriage was veering wildly off the tracks from the type of marriage he'd set out to secure. He'd certainly not planned such a scenario as that dinner. His stomach clenched. When she'd told him about her witch of a stepmother he'd wanted to smash something and lift her up into his arms, cursing the dead woman for making Samia ever doubt herself, for stopping her from doing what she'd so evidently loved. He'd wager a bet now that she had been a brilliant piano player.

He turned to survey the woman in the bed again, as if space could help him keep his hands off her. He almost laughed aloud at that. He'd never been so consumed with lust for anyone, and it perplexed him and sent tendrils of pure fear through him as well. It was like a primal need to stamp Samia as his. To ensure she never wanted to look at another man.

Sadiq went back towards the benignly sleeping figure on the bed and silently cursed her for not being the placid, unexciting, convenient wife he'd thought he'd signed up for.

The following morning, when the sun was high outside, Sadiq woke up to see Samia emerge from the shower, wrapping her robe around her. Immediately he felt disconcerted. He wasn't used to sleeping while in a woman's company—it had always made him feel intensely vulnerable. Yet another thing to add to the growing list of not so welcome experiences his wife was bringing into his life.

He put out a hand. 'You're overdressed. Come here so I can rectify the situation.'

She bit her lip and blushed, and immediately that tangled knot of emotions had Sadiq tensing all over. What was it about this woman?

Samia felt ridiculously nervous, and unaccountably weak

after a long night of being subjected to Sadiq's personal brand of torture. But she had to clarify something, because it was only afterwards she'd realised how arrogant he'd been.

She ignored his autocratic decree and said, 'Look, I would have appreciated talking about birth control before we...' She blushed and hitched up her chin. 'Before we made love. I think it is a good idea. If I'm already pregnant we'll know soon enough, but if I'm not then I'd prefer to use birth control for a few months at least.'

Sadiq was up on one arm, and to Samia's shock she saw a sheepish look cross his face before he smoothly got out of the bed and crossed to her. She tried to ignore his naked state and focus.

'I owe you an apology.'

'You do?'

'I should never have acted in such a cavalier manner. It was unbelievably arrogant and disrespectful to you. And, like I said, I *had* intended speaking with you about it.'

His easy apology made something melt inside her. Samia recalled the way it had felt to slide down on top of Sadiq, skin to skin, and between her legs she grew moist. If he could see inside her head she'd die of shame.

'It's fine. There was two of us there, and if I'd insisted you stop to use protection you would have.'

Sadiq tipped up her chin and with a rueful look in his eye said, 'I think you credit me with too much control—control which I seem to be in short supply of whenever you're near me.'

Samia's heart thumped once—hard. When Sadiq's eyes darkened and he opened her robe to push it from her shoulders she didn't protest.

CHAPTER TEN

THE next day Sadiq knew he was in very dangerous territory—literally and metaphorically. Samia was at the wheel of his Jeep and looking at him with a very mischievous grin on her face. They were teetering on the top of one of the steepest dunes he'd ever seen, and with not a little fear prickling his skin he cursed himself for giving in to her wish to drive. 'You do realise that if anything happens to me the Hussein line will die out?' he said.

Her grin got wider. 'Are you telling me you're scared?'

He was terrified. 'Never.'

She looked ahead, or more accurately down, and said in a grim voice, 'Hang on tight.'

And that was all Sadiq could do as they plunged down the sheer wall of sand. When they got to the bottom and he was still intact and breathing he opened one eye. Samia was already turning to climb back up the other side of the dune. She stopped the jeep and looked at him, 'See? Piece of cake. Next time we do it you can keep your eyes open.'

'I don't think so.' With awesome strength Sadiq lifted her from the driving seat and scooted over, so he was in control again. He smiled urbanely at Samia's pink indignant face. 'You've made your point. You've demonstrated your ability commendably. If I'm ever incapacitated in the desert I'd want no-one else to drive me out.'

She spluttered ineffectually as he expertly drove the Jeep back up the dune, and then finally he saw her smile out of the corner of his eye and heard something that sounded like, 'Honestly—*men*.'

The truth was that witnessing Samia's ability to dune-drive almost as expertly as he did, was making him feel off-centre. He wondered just how many more secrets she was hiding, along with that tantalising tattoo just above her plump buttocks. The thought of her buttocks made him change the gears awkwardly, grinding them painfully, and Sadiq took great pleasure in wiping the smug grin off Samia's face as they descended once again at an even more dangerous angle.

The following evening Sadiq was waiting for Samia when she came out of the bathroom. She felt a little dazed. They'd spent most of their time in bed, apart from one or two forays into the desert. She hadn't been dune-driving since she'd been a teenager with Kaden, and it had been exhilarating to surprise Sadiq with her proficiency. She'd forgotten the sheer joy there could be in that huge silent space. She'd seen a more carefree side to Sadiq than she would have believed existed—as if the desert injected him with some sort of re-laxant—and it had only been then that she'd realised how intensely he held himself in check all the time.

He was dressed in a long traditional robe and turban now, and looked slightly fearsome against the dusk. When she re-membered how expertly he'd handled his peregrine falcon earlier, and had stood behind her to show her how to hold him, she felt weak inside.

He smiled and flicked his eyes up and down, taking in the flimsy towel which was all she wore. Samia wished she had the confidence to let the towel drop and sashay over to him to seduce him, but he was indicating a box on the

bed and saying throatily, 'Change into those clothes and
then meet me downstairs. I want to take you somewhere
tonight.'

Wordlessly Samia watched him leave the room and
crossed to the bed. Opening the box, she gasped to find a gorgeous satin dress in a dark red colour. There was underwear
made of a material so fine it was like silk cobwebs. With
clumsy hands and a delicious sense of anticipation Samia
put the underwear on and let the dress drop down over her
head. Against her pale skin it looked sinful, and clung to
every curve before coming to rest on her feet.

She found matching shoes and put them on. They were so
high she teetered for a moment, before taking a deep breath
and leaving the room. Sadiq was waiting in the impressively
unadorned hall. Flame lanterns lit the ancient walls. As she
came down the stairs his eyes widened and the beat of her
heart got loud in her ears.

She came to a stop just feet away and he took her hand to
lead her ouside. He didn't say anything, but his eyes glowed
fiercely blue. Suddenly she realised something and embarrassment coursed through her.

She stopped and Sadiq looked back, impatience etched
into his features. 'What is it?'

Samia touched her hair and her face. 'I never did anything...with my hair or face. No makeup.'

She could have slid right into the ground. What kind of
a woman was she? What kind of woman just *forgot* parts
of getting ready? Alia had put together a vanity case full of
makeup and hair accessories for Samia. Samia didn't know
what to do with half of them, but she could have put on some
mascara, or lipstick, or something.

Sadiq came close and took her face in his hands. Samia
could see his impatience up close now and trembled—

because it was an impatience that echoed through her own body. An impatience to be naked and alone.

'You are absolutely stunning exactly as you are. I don't want you to change one thing. You don't need one shred of makeup.'

And then he kissed her so thoroughly that Samia knew that even if she had remembered to put lipstick on it would be well and truly gone by now. Mesmerised by his intensity, she let herself be guided into a more luxurious Jeep than the one they'd used for the dune-driving, and Sadiq drove them for about fifteen minutes in the darkening night before she saw flickering lights ahead. She was aware of the security Jeep and bodyguards behind them, but they were discreet.

She gasped when she saw what the lights were. An ornate bedouin tent, with a single palm tree and a small shimmering pool lit by the light of the full moon and flaming torches. It was beautiful—like something out of a fantasy.

Sadiq stopped the Jeep and cast her a glance. 'It's probably the smallest oasis in the world.'

Samia was already clambering out of the Jeep. 'It's perfect,' she breathed.

She took off her shoes so she could walk in the sand, and squealed when Sadiq lifted her up into his arms. He looked down at her with mock annoyance. 'You fool. Have you forgotten how dangerous it is to walk in the sand at night in bare feet?'

Samia scowled back at him. 'You're the one that gave me six inch heels. How am I supposed to walk in them?'

He grimaced. 'You're right. That was a stupid idea. I should have got you walking boots.'

Samia giggled to think of the incongruity of boots with this dress, and wiggled her toes deliciously. She cocked her head on one side. 'No, actually, I think I prefer being carried by you. Much more satisfying.'

And then, after a look so hot she wondered how she didn't go up in flames, Sadiq took her into the tent, and she had no sense of what was about to happen.

The sheer luxurious opulence of the scene took Samia's breath away and hit her between the eyes like a sledgehammer. Her heart started thumping, hard. It was like a scene from one of her childhood storybooks. The ones with pictures of sultans and Sheikhs sitting on sumptuous cushions eating delicacies, with beautiful exotic women reclining on equally luxurious divans.

She'd never even realised she held such a vision in her head. It was as if Sadiq was seeing right inside her to a secret place she hadn't been aware of herself, where she harboured a romantic fantasy of an idyll such as this, and was reproducing it with an ease that was truly awesome.

She tensed all over against the need to believe that this was real. When of course it couldn't be. Not in the way she wanted it to be—and that was a very scary revelation. It was as if she were freefalling from a great height; this whole scene was making her feel weak with yearning when it shouldn't.

An easy intimacy had stolen over Samia in the past few days, and she'd grown used to waking entwined with Sadiq, relishing his possessive embrace. But he'd warned her that he wasn't the cuddly type. He was just doing it for her benefit, for the honeymoon. It was all an act. It had to be. The man was a consummate seducer—he knew what women wanted. Was he doing this for her because he thought she needed it? Did he see the pathetic crush she was developing on him?

He finally put her down on her feet and she felt dizzy

and a little sick. Before she could make a complete fool of herself, or have him make some teasing sardonic comment, she asked in a quiet voice, 'Why are you doing this, Sadiq? You don't have to. We're married. You don't have to seduce me like this.'

'You don't have to seduce me like this.'

Sadiq felt as if he'd just been slapped in the face. He had that awful anxiety dream sensation of standing in front of a crowd of people and suddenly forgetting what he was meant to say, with everyone looking at him expectantly.

For the past few days something had stolen over him, seducing him. An intimacy he'd never experienced before. He'd found himself wanting to go deeper into the desert with Samia. Experience the vast openess with *her*. And, without even thinking about what he was doing, he'd arranged for this tent to be set up.

And now he felt foolish, exposed, because he suddenly realised how this must look. No wonder she was wondering what was going on. Why would she expect something like this? She wasn't a mistress, expecting such grand gestures. She hadn't even thought to put makeup on earlier—and why would she? She wasn't trying to entice Sadiq. They were *married*.

Suddenly absurdly angry with himself, Sadiq said harshly, 'Let's go back, then. It was a stupid idea.'

He was turning around when he felt his arm being pulled, and looked down to find himself diving into those blue depths. 'No, wait—I'm sorry. It's so beautiful. I'm just a bit confused…that's all. I'm not sure what this is.' Before he could accuse her of thinking it, Samia said in a rush, 'This is what you do for a lover, to seduce and entice, so what's the point, Sadiq?'

Sadiq's jaw clenched hard. He never acted out of blind

instinct. He was always completely aware of what he was doing and why. The enormity of what he'd done sank into him and the urge to self-protect became paramount.

He pulled her into his body, where she could feel the hard ridge of his erection. Much to his chagrin, nothing could dampen *that*. 'That's the point,' he ground out, pressing her closer, seeing how her eyes went dark with desire.

'If it makes you feel better then I'll tell you that I've brought all my mistresses here, so really it's been no bother. I fancied a change of scenery. That's all.'

Furious at the hurt that lanced her, mixed with relief that she hadn't given herself away, Samia said caustically, 'You're right. That does make me feel *so* much better. I'd hate to think you went to all this trouble just for me.'

Within seconds they were kissing furiously. Samia heard her dress rip when Sadiq pulled it open but she didn't care. All she cared about was that this mad, heated insanity was distracting her from something that felt very painful.

Their lovemaking was fast and furious, on one of the decadently sumptuous divans. When it was over Sadiq rolled away from Samia and she realised that he hadn't even fully undressed. She felt like apologizing, but the words were stuck in her throat. She could have said nothing, but she'd been so afraid of wanting to believe that this meant *something* she'd had to prove that it didn't. And she'd got her proof. Spectacularly.

Sadiq got up and rearranged his clothing. He barely glanced at Samia, who lay in what looked like wanton disarray. With a jerk of his head he said, 'There's a washing area behind the screen. When you're ready we'll go back to the castle. This was a mistake.'

Again Samia wanted to reach out and say... What? It was useless. She gathered up her dress and went behind the screen. The poor dress was so torn that Samia had to pull on a robe instead. When she emerged Sadiq was standing dressed in the doorway of the tent, the line of his back remote. It was only when Samia was walking towards the entrance that she saw the wine bucket with a bottle of champagne, two glasses, and a range of finger food delicacies.

She cursed herself for not keeping her mouth shut. Of *course* it wouldn't have meant anything—why had she had to insist on hearing that from Sadiq himself?

The next morning Sadiq stood looking out over the dawn breaking. The sight had never failed to take his breath away but this morning it was failing. Spectacularly. For some reason the desert had lost its effortless allure and it felt flat and drained of colour. And he wanted to see the back of it, which was entirely unlike him. No matter what was going on he always managed to find solace in this place.

He closed his eyes but it was no good. All he could see was Samia, holding that torn dress in her hands, and the way she'd walked with such regal hauteur back into the castle last night. It hadn't stopped him following her into the shower, though, and making love to her. The anger had still been simmering inside him, even though he'd known there was no rational reason for it. If anything, Samia had done him a favour in questioning his motives. Reminding him of what this was: a marriage of convenience.

He felt clammy now, recalling that initial feeling of exposure. What on earth had he been thinking of, organising the tent in the first place? Had his brain been so warped by a little dune driving and the hottest sex he'd ever had? Evidently.

The ironic thing about that blasted tent was that for years he'd had it in the back of his head to create some scene of seduction in the desert for his mistresses. More than one had asked him wistfully when he was going to take her to a secret desert oasis. And he never had, because at the last moment they'd always been the wrong person to share the desert with. And now the first woman he *had* brought to a secret desert oasis had all but thrown it back in his face.

He heard a rustle of movement behind him and turned slowly to face his wife, not liking the way he had to steel himself against the inevitable effect of seeing her.

Samia woke and was disorientated to see Sadiq standing looking out over the desert, fully dressed in traditional robes. For a silent moment she regarded his impressive back, and hated the ache at the back of her throat that signalled unshed tears. She was still angry when she thought of that tent, and the fact that Sadiq had seduced hundreds of women there. And, not only that, she hadn't been able to keep up her icy disdain when they'd returned to the castle. He'd arrogantly interrupted her shower and within seconds she'd been putty in his hands, slave to his masterful touch.

As if he could feel the weight of her gaze now, Sadiq turned around. Trying to look as composed and unmoved by him as she could, she came up on one arm, pushing her tangled hair over her shoulder. Self-conscious, and hating herself for it because she desperately craved to appear insouciant, she pulled the sheet up over her breasts.

He noted the movement with a small mocking smile, and Samia longed desperately to see him unsure of himself—just once.

He was cool. 'Something's come up in B'harani that needs my attention, I'm afraid we'll have to cut our time here a little short.'

Surprise, surprise, Samia thought, and said equally coolly, 'You should have woken me.'

Sadiq crossed his arms and rested back against the wall. 'I was enjoying the view too much.'

Recalling that she'd woken with the sheet barely covering her lower half, Samia gave up any pretence of nonchalance and jumped out of the bed, wrapping the sheet around her to go to the bathroom. She heard a dark chuckle, and had to restrain herself from flinging something at Sadiq's head when he stopped at the door to inform her that he'd be waiting downstairs.

The journey back to B'harani was made largely in silence, for which Samia was grateful. She felt absurdly over-emotional. Raw. When they reached the castle she jumped out of the Jeep and only stopped when she heard her name. Tense all over, she turned to see Sadiq, with a bevy of aides and advisers descending on him from all sides.

He looked stern, and already more remote. 'I'll be working late tonight so don't wait up.'

'Don't worry, Sadiq,' she said as loftily as she could. 'I don't expect you to entertain me. The honeymoon is over.'

She turned away, but he called her name again. Softly. This time when she turned he was much closer and her heart sputtered. She looked up to see a feral glitter in his eyes and the answering effect on her body was instantaneous. 'I asked for you to be moved to my rooms Samia, so make sure you have everything you need.'

Immediately she felt threatened. She'd forgotten, and the thought of coping with Sadiq every night was suddenly too much—especially feeling as raw as she did right now. She opened her mouth. 'Actually, I'm not sure that I—'

Sadiq put a finger to her lips and said with a steel tone, 'It's non-negotiable, Samia.'

And then he turned and was swallowed up by the crowd of people.

Sadiq was burningly aware of Samia's huge eyes boring into his back as he walked down the long corridor away from her, and he had to battle the urge to turn around, pick her up and take her straight to bed. He had to control himself— quash this urge to want to punish Samia for something. For making him *feel*? For making him fearful of the passion she inspired in him because it was making him act in ways he'd never done before, becoming irrational and impulsive? Just like his father?

Sadiq immediately dismissed the notion as ridiculous. But as the rogue thought was sinking in and taking up residence Sadiq's steps quickened perceptibly, and the retinue of staff almost had to run to keep up with him.

A week later Samia was fired up and full of enthusiasm. She was determined to block out the fact that the distance between her and Sadiq since they'd returned from Nazirat seemed to be growing into a wedge. She assured herself that he was busy, catching up on work he'd had to sideline for the marriage. And what had she expected anyway? Romantic dinners *à deux* every night? Hadn't she told him in no uncertain terms in Nazirat that he didn't have to do that?

In the bedroom, however, there was no distance. She blushed now as she walked along the long corridor to Sadiq's offices to think of how passionate he'd been last night. She'd been half asleep when he'd come to bed, but had soon been wide awake when she'd felt his firm, hard body curling around hers. It scared her how a warm glow seemed to infuse every cell whenever he was near or touched her. And the way everything semed to dim when he wasn't.

She tried to tell herself that she didn't miss the way he'd pulled her close after making love those first few days in Nazirat. She tried to tell herself that it didn't hurt to know that it had all just been an act for the honeymoon. Now, when they made love, Sadiq rolled away, and Samia hated the longing she felt to snuggle close, feel his arms around her. She cursed him for ever giving her that experience, so that she could miss it. Some mornings, though, she woke with the sensation that he'd held her during the night. But invariably Sadiq would already be gone, and that was always a stark reminder that they had moved very definitely into the 'convenient' part of their marriage.

Determined to stop this dangerous line of thinking, stop obsessing over Sadiq like some groupie, Samia had got up today determined to discuss with Sadiq some ideas she had that she wanted to develop and work on. When she got to the anteroom of his office, and his secretary looked up and smiled, Samia had to quash the sudden yearning to be able to just walk blithely into his office simply because he would always want to welcome her, to see her.

Oh, Lord. She almost stumbled when the implication of what she was thinking sank in. She couldn't deal with it now. She smiled back at the efficient secretary, pristine in a long white tunic and colourful veil.

'Do go in, Queen Samia. He's got a few minutes between meetings.'

Samia knocked lightly and heard Sadiq's deep voice respond. Immediately silly little butterflies started in her belly and she cursed. Opening the door, she went in and was surprised not to see Sadiq behind a mountain of paperwork. He was standing at the window, looking very brooding.

He turned around and black brows drew together in a frown. No hint of pleasure to see her. Samia cursed herself again, and hated that she felt her old sense of insecurity come back. 'I...I'm sorry to disturb you. I wanted to discuss a couple of things with you.'

Sadiq flicked a glance at his watch and Samia felt it like a slap. He was dressed in a suit today, and it reminded Samia of when she'd first seen him in London, which felt like aeons ago. He was so remote that she almost wondered if he was the same man who had made tears of pleasure soak her cheeks last night. Who had used his thumbs to wipe them away while they were still intimately joined. As if loath to let him leave her body she had jealously gripped his hips with her thighs, as if to stop him ever leaving.

She swayed for a moment because the memory was so potent, and instantly Sadiq was at her side, his frown even more fierce, 'Are you all right?'

'Fine...' Aghast at her own wayward imagination, Samia pulled free and walked over to a chair, saying much more brightly, 'I'm fine. I know you're busy.'

Sadiq had walked back behind his desk and sat down, once more cool and remote, as if that little moment hadn't ocurred. The stark reality that this would be their everyday lives made her feel slightly panicky. Which got worse when he said, 'I have ten minutes.'

Samia sat down primly. Sadiq's office was huge and unahamedly masculine. Dark wood and shelves lined with books. She blurted out. 'I'd like an office.'

'You have an office.'

Samia thought of the perfectly nice room which was essentially somewhere for her to use the internet and make phone calls. She shook her head. 'No, I mean I want a proper office—like this. Where I can put my books and work on projects.'

He arched a brow and sat back, but Samia sensed the danger in his indolence. 'Projects?'

She nodded. 'Yes. You mentioned your environmental projects before. I'd like to see how I can help. And I want to set up some kind of literacy programme. Al-Omar is like Burquat in the fact that free education was only recently introduced—when you became Sultan. It was the same with my brother. The older generations who missed out have very low literacy. I'd like to set up workshops to encourage people to come back to school.'

Sadiq was looking at her with a funny expression on his face but she decided to forge on. 'And I want to set up a crèche here in the castle. There is no facility to help female staff to continue working once they've had a child, and you employ more women than men.'

Sadiq's jaw tensed. 'Anything else?'

Samia shrugged. 'Lots of things… But I'd like to start with those for now.'

Sadiq felt immediately defensive at having things pointed out to him that he'd already been aware of but hadn't really looked at yet, due to more pressing concerns. And he was also reacting to the fact that once again Samia was proving she wouldn't be morphing seamlessly into the role he'd envisaged his wife taking. He'd seen his wife firmly in the background, merely enhancing his role and perhaps attending some social events in his place. He hadn't really seen his marriage as a working partnership, and his naivety and lack of foresight mocked him now.

Self-recrimination made his voice harsh. 'The charity circuit is a well-oiled and sophisticated machine in B'harani, and there are plenty of committees of which you will have automatically become chairperson. I think, if you look at the schedule laid out for you, you'll be kept quite busy.'

Samia had looked at that schedule at the start of the week and her heart had sunk. She'd been spurred into action, doing her own research. She stood up on a wave of hot anger. 'I don't want to sit on committees to talk about things and never do them. And, as valuable as the charity circuit is, I want to do something useful—not just be a figurehead while other people do the work. I'm perfectly prepared to put in the hours being seen, but that's not enough.'

Sadiq stood too, and put his hands on the table, not liking

the way he was thinking of Samia's insecurity around crowds and being seen, and how much it moved him to see the way she seemed so determined not to let it get to her. He felt something harden inside him, and knew he was reacting to the increasingly familiar sense of threat this woman posed.

'This is not the time nor the place for this discussion, Samia, but there is one thing to consider—what happens when we have children?'

Samia gritted her jaw, dismayed and disappointed to see this hitherto hidden traditional side of Sadiq. 'If and when we have children I would expect to be able to use the crèche facility which has been set up, and in doing so demonstrate that we're rulers of the people who do not see themselves as unapproachable. And I would continue doing as much important work as I could—just as you would.'

Samia was articulating what Sadiq himself would have agreed with on any other occasion and with any other person. But here, with *her* and all the ambiguous feelings she aroused, Sadiq was frigid. 'Tell me, have you already sought out an area for this crèche?'

Samia was determined not to be intimidated. 'I have, actually, and there is a perfect spot near to the staff entrance of the castle. It's got a green area, which could be developed into a playground, and there's a huge bright room which could be converted from the storeroom it currently is.'

Sadiq instantly knew where she was talking about, and it did have potential. But for some reason he felt compelled to shoot it all down. He was reacting viscerally again, and hated that he was, but couldn't seem to stop it. He wanted to relegate Samia to some place where he wouldn't have to deal with her. Much as he had all week. Avoiding any contact by day and then using the nights to let his already shaky control go.

Each morning he'd woken up and hoped for some sense

that clarity was returning, or her sensual hold over him was diminished, but if the way his body felt so hot and hard right now was anything to go by he was in for a long wait. 'I've been running this country on my own for well over a decade, Samia. You will fulfil the role of my queen. I don't need a wife with a busier schedule than my own. I don't want you starting something off only to grow bored with it, leaving it to overworked staff to finish off.'

Samia was shaking she was so incensed. 'I wouldn't do that. You chose *me* to be your wife and I'm not going to settle for a life of posturing and preening.' To her utter horror, she felt tears threaten. 'You *know* I'm not like that. I told you from the very start and you wouldn't listen. I can be useful and I intend to be.'

Terrified she'd start crying in front of him, and of the emotion gripping her, Samia turned around and rushed from the room. She walked with tears blurring her vision until she found a quiet spot, and then hid away and tried to stifle the gulping, shuddering breaths. She knew exactly why she was so upset. The realisation had started to hit her outside Sadiq's office. She had fallen in love with her husband, and all of those iron-clad assertions that she would never be so stupid had just crumbled to dust.

She was upset because she'd gone in there today hoping… for what? she asked herself angrily as she wiped at her stinging cheeks. That he would jump up and tell her how brilliant she was? What amazing ingenuity she had? She'd been naive to think he would just allow her free rein to do what she liked.

He was right. He'd been running the country very successfully, *alone*, for a long time. He was hardly likely to welcome a couple of bright ideas along with a rush of enthusiasm as something solid to work on. But she was hurt that he didn't know her well enough by now to know that she wouldn't be so inconsistent as to start something and not finish it.

Composing herself, Samia left her hiding place and went to find Yasmeena, whom she'd promised to have lunch with that day. She hoped that the surprisingly astute woman wouldn't notice her turmoil.

Samia reassured herself stoutly that she couldn't have fallen in love with Sadiq. She was mistaken. She was over-emotional, that was all. She nearly stumbled, though, when she thought again of the crèche and had an image of Sadiq bending down to scoop up a dark haired toddler from the sandpit.

For a moment the pain was so intense that Samia thought she might have to make up some excuse and avoid lunch, but exerting all her self-control, she pasted a bright smile on her face and kept going.

A couple of days later Samia was in her office, looking at the schedule of events, and fear was rising within her. Next week was to be the start of her official duties, as the marriage festivities and honeymoon period were formally finished. This was a schedule of daytime events, and was considered part of her queenly duties—*alone*. She wouldn't have Sadiq's solid presence by her side. She could already picture the charity/ social scene brigade of women who orchestrated these events and she shuddered. They would assess her in an instant and find her lacking.

Just then her door opened and Sadiq filled the space, broad shoulders blocking out the light. Samia felt that awful rush of emotion and dampened it down. She was still angry with him. She had wanted to be able to turn her back on him when he'd come to bed the previous nights, but with awful predictability within seconds she'd been incapable of remembering her name, never mind saying no to Sadiq.

Conversation had been nil, but Samia had woken up during the night and found herself wrapped tightly in Sadiq's embrace. She'd stayed awake for a long time, relishing the contact she knew he'd break free of as soon as he woke.

She strove for cool uninterest now. 'Can I help you?'

Sadiq's mouth twitched ever so slightly and Samia flushed. Even now he was laughing at her. But then he strode in and her mind blanked. He plucked the sheet of paper she'd been studying out of her hands and perused it, before calmly tearing it in two.

Samia looked open-mouthed from it to Sadiq. 'What did you do that for?'

'Because your secretary is going to draw you up a new schedule and it'll consist only of the events that you wish to go to.'

Samia repeated stupidly, 'Secretary? I don't have a secretary.'

Sadiq indicated for Samia to get up and follow him, and said, 'You do now. It sounds like you're going to be busy enough to need one.'

Struck dumb, Samia followed Sadiq out of the room and into another one, much bigger, just down the hall. It was bright and airy, and the castle workmen who were busy putting up shelves stopped working and bowed deferentially.

Sadiq said brusquely, 'Leave us, please, for a moment.'

The men filed out and Samia turned around. There was a huge desk, complete with computer, printer, fax machine. A small anteroom was obviously the secretary's office.

She was almost too scared to look at Sadiq—afraid of what he might see on her face. 'What is this…? Why have you done this?'

He sighed and she looked up. His face was unreadable. 'The truth is that I did have a preconceived notion of the role my wife would fulfil, and was quite happy to acknowledge

that it wouldn't impinge on my own role at all. Merely enhance it.' He smiled tightly. 'I should have known that you
wouldn't be happy with that. I like your ideas. And I'm sorry
for doubting your ability to start them and finish them. I
watched my father do that for years—when he died and I
took over he'd left behind him a trail of destruction and half
finished projects. I vowed not to let that happen again. I've
wielded control for so long that it's challenging to allow myself to hand some of it over now.'

More moved than she wanted to show, Samia said quietly,
'I thought this marriage would be a partnership…apart from
everything else.'

'It is, Samia. I want you to be happy here.'

Samia's heart ached at his gesture, and ached in a different way at his impersonal words. She wouldn't be truly
happy here unless a miracle happened and the block of ice
in Sadiq's chest melted. But this was a start. She smiled, and
her heart thumped when she saw his eyes flare. They had
chemistry too, and that was something to build on.

Feeling optimistic for the first time in days, Samia said
simply, 'Thank you. I appreciate this, and I won't let you
down.'

Sadiq felt a physical pain somewhere in the region of
his chest at the sheer happiness in Samia's face. And he
felt better than he had in days. A black mood had pervaded
his whole being ever since their last exchange, and his con-
science hadn't allowed him to continue functioning until
he'd rectified the situation.

Before Samia could see how her happiness seemed to
be having a disturbing effect on him, he grabbed the two
hard hats he'd left on the desk earlier and handed one to her.
'Come on. I've something else to show you.'

A few minutes later Samia couldn't stop the tears from
stinging her eyes. Sadiq had brought her to the back of the

castle, where construction work was already starting on a crèche and playground. That potent image of Sadiq and a little toddler rose up again and wouldn't leave her alone. It was like a taunt.

When Sadiq turned and saw her glistening eyes, and asked sharply, 'What is it?' Samia panicked and muttered something about grit getting in her eye.

To her utter surprise Sadiq immediately picked her up into his arms and, despite her heated remonstrations that she was fine, took her straight to the castle's full-time nurse. Samia was brick-red with mortification, absolutely certain that the nurse would see full well that she'd just been crying and had lied shamefully. But to her abject relief Sadiq said he had to go to a meeting and left her saying something about working late. Samia was too distracted to care.

It was only when she lay in bed alone that night that she frowned slightly, trying to remember that Sadiq had said. A little dart of emotion made her breath hitch. The fact was he'd done a great thing today, and changed the anatomy of their marriage and Samia's role within it in one fell swoop. But apart from that, the distance between them was as great as ever.

Sadiq didn't seem remotely interested in involving Samia in any aspect of his life that wasn't about sex or official duties. There was no suggestion of dinner, or meeting for lunch. No suggestion of a *relationship*. And why should there be? she remonstrated with herself. She was the one yearning for more, not him. He'd got exactly what he wanted from this marriage, even if she was demanding a bigger role than he would have expected or liked.

But she couldn't help thinking back to those few days of the honeymoon, when it had felt as if they'd really been getting to know one another. Samia had enjoyed spending time with him. They'd talked. But she didn't need to be reminded that their conversation over dinner when he'd told her about his father had been their last conversation of any depth or substance. Clearly that had been an aberration that Sadiq had no intention of repeating.

Samia finally fell asleep, and tried not to mind very much that she had no idea where Sadiq was.

CHAPTER ELEVEN

THREE weeks later Sadiq was sitting in his study with a glass of whisky in his hand. He grimaced at himself. This was becoming a habit. Work until his vision blurred, wait around, and then go to bed. Invariably when Samia was already asleep or half asleep.

Each night he told himself he would be strong enough to resist her lure, that he wasn't some animal, a slave to his base instincts, but when he pulled back the covers and saw those delicate curves…that long hair…fire consumed him and he jumped into the pit. Every night. And she gave with the wild abandon he'd grown addicted to every night.

He grimaced again. Since when had his shy wife grown so *un*-shy that she felt comfortable sleeping naked? The thought of her now, naked in the bed, made him grip the glass so tight that it cracked in his palm. Sadiq saw the trickle of blood fall on his robe, and for a moment pain blocked out the ever-present awareness, and he had an insight into why people might seek pain as a sort of anaesthetic.

He smiled at his own bleak humour and got up to tend to his cut. The good mood he'd been in for days after showing Samia her new office, telling her that she had *carte blanche* to do pretty much whatever she liked, was wearing off and being replaced with something much darker and more insidious.

It didn't help that he was well aware that he was doing his utmost to avoid spending any time with his wife. Because whenever he was alone with her he couldn't think straight. All rational thought went out of the window and he found himself filled with bizarre longings that had nothing to do with lust—although that was ever-present—and more to do with something more intangible. Like the urge he'd had in Nazirat to take Samia deep into the desert.

It was too reminiscent of the moods he'd seen grip his father. What more evidence did he need than the fact he was breaking glasses in his hand just thinking of Samia? She was dangerous.

Sadiq patched up his hand and caught a glimpse of his reflection in the mirror. His eyes were glittering as if he had a fever. His jaw was stubbled with a day's growth of beard. He looked a little wild. He suddenly realised that this situation was untenable, and a surge of anger at Samia and her innocently sleeping presence made him switch off the light and stride from his study.

The following evening Samia was looking at her pink face in the steamed-up bathroom mirror. She knew it was crazy to feel disappointed—the chasm that currently existed between her and Sadiq was no place to be bringing a baby. If she'd thought that his *volte-face* about her involvement in their marriage had signified a change, then she'd been mistaken. If anything, Sadiq was growing even more distant. She put her hand to her flat belly and bit her lip. She'd just seen the spotting which signified that she wasn't pregnant.

She heard him moving in the bedroom outside and tensed. They were going to a function being held in the castle that evening—an acknowledgement of Sadiq's fundraising for charities. Taking a deep breath, she tightened the robe around her body and went out. Sadiq was stripping off his shirt and immediately Samia's pulse went into overdrive.

He caught her look and his mouth curled. 'Don't look at me like that, *habiba*. We don't have time to make something of it.'

Samia flushed, and flushed even harder when she thought of how their lovemaking last night had been imbued with something almost desperate. She'd only noticed the make-shift bandage on Sadiq's hand afterwards, and the red stain of blood. Her heart clenching, she'd asked, 'What happened?'

He'd taken his hand back and said brusquely, 'Nothing. Just a glass that broke.'

And, practically jackknifing off the bed, he'd then informed her that he'd just remembered a speech he had to work on, and pulled on some clothes and gone back to his office. Samia knew he'd only returned to their bedroom to shower that morning. So he must have slept in his office.

She thought of that now, and wanted to feel relief as she said, 'There's something I should tell you.'

He looked at her, naked now apart from form-fitting boxers that held a distinctive bulge.

Samia swallowed. She had to get sex off her brain. 'I'm not pregnant.'

For a long moment Sadiq was silent. She couldn't read his reaction. And then he just calmly pulled on his pants and said, 'Good. That's good. Thank you for letting me know.' His eyes flicked her up and down and she felt it like the lash of a whip. 'We're leaving in twenty minutes.'

Chin hitched up, Samia said, 'I'll be ready.'

And she was—with not a hint of her reaction on her face to his emotionless response to the news that she wasn't pregnant.

An hour later Sadiq was still coming to grips with the fact that he'd felt disappointed to hear that Samia wasn't pregnant—as if something elusive had slipped out of his grasp. He'd had an almost primal urge to make love to her when she'd said that, as if to ensure that she *did* get pregnant when she'd expressly told him she didn't want that.

He felt weak, at the mercy of something he had no control over. She'd taken his injured hand in hers last night, and the feel of those small cool hands had provoked an urge to put his head on Samia's breast and have her hold him. It had been strong enough to make him run. And he'd spent the night on the couch in his office, waking with a dry mouth and in a foul humour that was getting fouler by the minute.

Especially when he saw Samia across the room, laughing up into the face of a handsome man whom Sadiq recognised as one of his scientists involved in environmental research. He knew Samia had been having meetings with them last week, and to think she was cultivating a relationship—no matter how innocent—with this man was enough to propel him across the room in seconds. He took Samia's arm in his hand, relishing the feel of the delicate muscles. She was *his*. The other man backed away hurriedly, as if Sadiq had just snarled at him like an animal.

He heard Samia's husky voice. 'Sadiq? Is everything okay?'

He looked down at her and something solidified inside him. 'No,' he bit out grimly. 'Everything is not okay.'

Samia watched him locking the door behind them. He'd all but marched her into an empty anteroom, and the fierce look on his face scared her slightly. 'What's going on, Sadiq?'

'What's going on is that I leave your side for two minutes and you're flirting with another man.'

She gaped at him. 'Flirting? I can assure you that I was

not flirting. Hamad was telling me about his two-year-old son, if you must know.'

Sadiq rocked back on his heels, hands in his pockets. He said almost musingly, but with a dangerous undercurrent, 'When we first met you would have had me believe that you'd be quaking in your shoes in a situation like that, and yet you're remarkably eager to leave my side and talk to relative strangers.'

Hurt scored Samia's insides. She wasn't about to let him know how vulnerable she still felt in those situations, or why the only reason she felt she could deal with them was because he was by her side, or nearby. Even just to see him across a room was enough.

She tossed her head, knowing she was playing with fire. 'Are you accusing me of lying, Sadiq? Pretending that I was shy and insecure? And am I not *meant* to leave your side? I thought part of my brief as your queen of convenience was to *work*.'

She couldn't stop now. 'Because that's what this marriage is, isn't it, Sadiq? It's just a job, with a bit of sex thrown in. You can't even be bothered to pretend it's anything else and have *one* evening meal with me. We have nothing to discuss.'

Sadiq moved fast enough to shock Samia. He was right in front of her, saying harshly, 'You've certainly shown me intriguing facets to your personality that weren't in evidence when we first met.' His eyes were bright with a feral glitter as they dropped down and took in where her cleavage was revealed in the silk of the simple dress. 'And there's *plenty* we could discuss, Samia.'

She took a step back, railing against the evidence that he resented the aspects of her that had started to emerge as if from a long hibernation, and fought the dismayingly familiar lure to merge with this man. 'I'm not talking about sex,

Sadiq. I'm talking about the fact that you want an identikit wife and that's not what I am.'

Her voice was bitter. 'Obviously you'd prefer it if I'd stayed shy and gauche, but you're the one who has been encouraging me to overcome that shyness. You can't have it both ways, Sadiq. Perhaps there's no point to this marriage if you can't see that?'

He went very still. 'What are you saying? That you want out?'

Samia blinked. It felt as if they had jumped about three levels up from where she'd thought they were. For the first time in years she stuttered. 'N-no. I mean, I d-don't know. I didn't mean that. I just mean that we don't seem to have anything—' she blushed '—but the sex.'

The stutter got him right in the gut. That glaring sign of vulnerability underneath the thin veneer of bravado made something break inside Sadiq. His anger was defused and he saw in an instant how hard she was trying. He also recognised that she was all of the things she'd been that first day she'd met him and yet was also the emerging strong woman who had been repressed for so long.

She was the woman who still clung on to his hand with a death grip for the first few minutes in a crowded room until she was comfortable enough to leave his side. She was the woman with the tattoo above her buttocks, who could dune-drive and throw herself into the building of a crèche with so much enthusiasm that only last week he'd found her in dusty overalls, making sweet tea for the workers and laughing with them.

And she was the only woman he'd ever wanted to take deep into the desert and seduce in a bedouin tent erected just for her.

Panic and a feeling of constriction so strong that Sadiq had to stop himself undoing his bowtie forced him to speak the words that had just formed in his head from somewhere deep and dark inside him. 'If you want to leave this marriage, I'll give you a divorce.'

Samia looked at Sadiq, shock numbing her from the inside out. 'If *I* want to leave, you'll give me a divorce?'

He nodded, his face once again a mask of inscrutability.

Samia had the urge to slap him—hard. Feeling slightly desperate, she said, 'But I've committed to this marriage, to you. I'm learning to find my feet…I'm happy here.'

A voice mocked her. *Really? You're happy to be in this relationship with a man who doesn't love you and never will?*

Suddenly insecure in a way she hadn't felt for some weeks now, Samia looked at Sadiq, even though it was hard. '*You* want to divorce *me*.'

He shook his head. 'That's not what I'm saying. I'm offering you the choice. I'd be quite happy to stay married, but I don't think you're happy.' *Liar*, a voice mocked him. *You're going slowly insane.*

Samia wanted to sit down. 'Why?' she asked.

Sadiq sighed deeply and ran a hand through his hair, leaving it dishevelled. The muted chink of glasses and the hum of conversation from outside went unnoticed. 'Because you never wanted this marriage, and because I all but railroaded you into it. I don't relish the prospect of a wife who is going to feel she's in a situation she can't leave and grow to resent the feeling of being trapped. I watched my mother go through that and I won't be responsible for the same thing. I don't want to bring a child into that environment. Needless to say, if you do want to leave it won't affect my relationship with Burquat.'

'You've thought about this,' Samia said dully, the pain of that making her want to curl up somewhere.

Sadiq curbed the urge to contradict her. It seemed to be

a very simple equation in his head—hand Samia every tool or reason she might need to leave and she would leave. And he would feel sane again.

'What if I don't want to leave?'

There was something slightly defiant in her tone, and it made Sadiq alternately panicked and euphoric. Angry at the fact that she was once again confounding his expectations, he said, 'You'll have to come to terms with what this marriage is, Samia. Unless things have changed for you this is still an arranged marriage, and we are together for many reasons—none of which is about love. So I can't guarantee to be more invested than I already am.'

Every word landed on Samia like a little bomb. It was as if she'd asked silently for him to really spell it out, because she wasn't quite sure what he meant. To save herself from the final humiliation, she said coolly, 'I know what the parameters of this marriage are, Sadiq, but I'd hoped that within that we could find some balance where we at least communicated beyond the bedroom.'

Sadiq gritted out, 'We're communicating now.'

'Yes, and it's very clear. Can I have some time to think about this?'

Sadiq felt unsteady for a moment, unsettled by Samia's composure. 'Of course. This isn't something that has to be decided any time soon.'

'It's good to know there's no pressure.'

Sadiq heard the sarcasm dripping from her voice, and watched as his wife walked straight-backed to the door, turned the key and went back outside. He felt all at once light-headed, panicky and as if something incredibly precious was slipping away.

When he got back to the main ballroom, though, and saw Samia standing talking to the same man he'd seen her with before, Sadiq cursed himself for giving her an option to leave at all. He should be divorcing her point-blank—because that was the only solution to this madness.

CHAPTER TWELVE

Sᴀᴅɪǫ paced impatiently in his office and checked his watch again. Where the hell was she? Samia had told him that morning that she would come and talk to him this afternoon. As the days had passed during the past week, and Samia had gone about her business as serenely as if nothing had happened, his control had become more and more frayed. Nerves wound to breaking point.

The self-enforced sleepless nights on his couch in his study had provoked some much needed introspection. At first Sadiq had tried to block it out with alcohol, but in the end, disgusted with himself, he'd lain there and thought— really thought—about what he would do if Samia wanted to divorce, and why he'd offered it up as an option in the first place.

And then something his mother had said had hit home uncomfortably. Sick of trying to pace away his sexual frustration in his office, one morning he'd sought some air and space and had come across his mother, sitting in a quiet courtyard in the shade. He'd had that immediate reflex to leave, but in a firmer voice than she usually used she'd asked him to join her, so he had.

For the first time in a long time they'd sat in companionable silence, and finally she'd said, 'This place is changing by the day. Can't you feel it?'

He'd cast her a glance and she'd gone on, not looking at him. 'Your Samia—she's a breath of fresh air. Just what we've needed for a long time.'

The way the words *your Samia* had impacted on Sadiq had been nothing short of a block landing on his chest.

And then his mother had said quietly, 'It is possible, you know, to feel passion for someone and for it *not* to be a negative thing that has to be controlled. The difference is love. I had that once—before your father. The memory of it was the only thing that kept me sane. As well as you, of course.'

And with those engimatic words she'd got up, pressed a kiss to his head and left him sitting there, reeling. Finally seeing things clearly for the first time in weeks.

The phone rang on Sadiq's desk now, and he snatched it up, answering curtly, 'Yes?' He couldn't hide his impatience, but went very still as he listened to the voice on the other end.

After a pause he said, distractedly, 'Yes…thank you…I will.'

He put down the phone. A mixture of emotions was making him feel dizzy, but the paramount one was abject relief. Samia couldn't leave him now, even if she wanted to. He would deal with the matter of whether she wanted to or not when he found her.

Samia knew she should have been in Sadiq's study ages ago, but she couldn't see him while she was still a sniveling, quivering wreck. Ever since she'd discovered the reason for her persistant nausea all week the tears hadn't seemed to stop.

She groaned out loud as she blew her nose again. She had to get it together so that she could stand before Sadiq's cool, sardonic presence and not crumble. She'd been so strong all week—numbing herself to the pain, alternating between thinking that she would tell Sadiq she'd stay in the marriage because the prospect of not seeing him was too hard to bear, and vowing to herself that there was no other option but to divorce him and run. Before her heart broke into tiny pieces and could never be put back together.

He'd even stopped sleeping with her, so evidently he was already getting used to single life again. That provoked a fresh bout of weeping, because it was futile thinking of this. It was all beside the point now.

She heard a noise behind her and whirled around to see Sadiq, leaning against the closed library door.

'How did you know where I was?'

'I figured you'd be in the one place you feel safest.'

Samia went pink. *Why* had she told him so much about herself? 'If you've come to accuse me of pretending to be something I'm not again, then—'

He moved forward, frowning. 'You're crying.'

'No, I'm not,' she lied, looking away.

But Sadiq kept coming until he was right in front of her, tipping her chin up so he could see her face. She gritted her jaw. He was so damned arrogant. But that familiar scent wound around her and she had to stop herself closing her eyes and drinking it in deeply.

Hating his effortless effect on her, when he could be so unmoved, Samia jerked away and wrapped her arms around herself. She was dressed in a long tunic and matching tight pants.

She wasn't prepared for what Sadiq said next. 'Are you upset because of the pregnancy?'

Shocked, Samia just looked at him. 'How do you know?'

'The doctor thought you had come straight to me to give me the news, so he rang with congratulations.'

'Oh…' Samia bit her lip.

He would now know that there was no way she could leave

the marriage. Afraid to see the trapped look in his eyes, she stared down at the carpet.

'I'm not upset because of the pregnancy.' She looked up again, steeling herself for whatever Sadiq's reaction would be. 'When the doctor told me, I was happy. Apparently spotting is common in the early days. My periods have always been light…that's why I assumed I wasn't pregnant.'

Sadiq's voice was firm. 'But you are. And that changes everything.'

Samia nodded miserably, and saw something flash in Sadiq's eyes. 'Are you upset because this means you can't leave our marriage?' he asked.

Samia blinked back the onset of more tears. She half shrugged, half nodded, and shook her head. 'No… I mean… yes. But not because of what you probably think.'

The enormity of discovering about the baby had stripped Samia's soul bare. She didn't have the energy to be anything less than completely honest now, and she would just have to cope with Sadiq's indifference as best she could. She had a baby to think about, and that was more important. She felt instinctively that Sadiq would be a good father.

'I'm upset, Sadiq, because I've fallen in love with you. I don't know what I would have told you today, but I would have chosen whichever option would make my heartbreak marginally less. I hadn't yet figured out if that meant leaving you or staying here. But now…' She put her hand on her belly. 'Now I don't even have the illusion of choice, and you're just going to have to deal with the fact that, even though you've given me every opportunity to dislike you intensely, I love you.'

Samia watched several expressions cross Sadiq's face: sheer disbelief, shock, wonder and something like the sun breaking out from behind stormy clouds. Her pathetic heart started to thump but she had to ignore it.

He came close to her again and she backed away, but hit a wall of books. He was smiling, but Samia felt like scowling. He put his hands on either side of her head and leant in, trapping her. Samia had a flashback to when she'd seen him kissing that woman in this very room all those years before. She couldn't believe she hadn't remembered it straight away.

'You're remembering, aren't you?'

Samia's eyes widened. 'Remembering what?' He couldn't possibly be talking about—

'That night—in here, at my party. When you were sitting in a chair in the dark, like a scared little mouse in glasses.'

'I—' Heat was pulsing through Samia. She'd been about to deny it. 'I was already here and you came in. And then that woman.'

Sadiq grimaced. 'Don't remind me.'

Samia was finding it hard to concentrate. She'd just told Sadiq she loved him and he hadn't responded. And now his pelvis was against hers and she could feel his burgeoning response. And he remembered her from that night.

His eyes were bluer than she could ever remember seeing them, and something imperceptible had softened in his face. It reminded her of when she'd seen him smile after dune-driving, with sheer exhilaration and joy.

'Sadiq—'

'Do you know why I remember that moment now?'

She shook her head. He took a long strand of her hair that had fallen over her shoulder and wound it round his finger. 'Because seeing you here in this room brought it back. I saw your embarrassed reaction to knocking over the table of drinks that night and in a split second you'd shown more emotion than I'd seen anyone show in years. It made me feel restless, unsatisfied. I was searching for something elusive that I'd never managed to find with any woman. A depth of passion. A depth of emotion. And the only person I have ever found that with is *you*. As soon as I walked in just now and saw your eyes I remembered that you'd been the silent witness to my isolation that night...' His smile faded slightly and his eyes were intense on hers. 'And the catalyst.'

Samia was wondering if she was dreaming. 'I wanted to come and say something, and then...*she* came in.'

Sadiq nodded. 'I felt like someone was watching me, and then when I turned around it was *her* and it felt all wrong. But then when we heard you...and I saw those big eyes just before you ran...I knew it had been you, and I sensed a kinship, a connection.'

Samia looked away. She wasn't dreaming. She was about to be humiliated. 'No, you didn't. You don't have to say that.'

He caught her chin and gently brought it back. He was deadly serious. 'Yes, I did. And, yes, I do have to say that— because from the day you walked into my office in London that connection was there. I have done my absolute best from that day to avoid acknowledging it. When the explosive chemistry between us became apparent I concentrated on that, determined not to admit that there could possibly be any emotional depth too.'

Feeling very shaky and exposed, Samia said, 'What are you saying, Sadiq?'

'What I'm saying, my love, *habibti*, is that I've been fathoms deep in love with you for weeks, but I've been too afraid to admit it to myself. The more you revealed your true self, the more I fell in love with you—and the more threatened I felt. It's been a perfect law of physics. The more you captured my heart, the more I had to push you away.'

Not wanting to believe this for a moment, because it was too huge, Samia said, 'You don't have to say this just because of the baby.'

Sadiq looked fierce enough to make her tremble. He put a possessive hand on her belly. 'From the moment the doctor told me about your pregnancy all my preconceived notions flew out of the window. I've never felt such pure joy. I want to bring this child up with love. It'll be my heir, yes, but he or she will be *ours*, first and foremost, and can do whatever they want. I was coming to find you to tell you exactly what I'm telling you, but then I found you crying and assumed you were upset because it meant you were trapped with me for ever.'

He shook his head. 'Forgive me for last week. I was so confused about how I was feeling I seriously believed for all of about twenty-four hours that encouraging you to divorce me was the solution. It was only when I stayed away from you and forced myself to see what that future would be like that I had to face up to myself.'

Samia felt very wobbly, and tears were pricking her eyes. 'Sadiq, I love you so much. If you're just saying this—I don't think I could cope if you don't really mean it.'

He took her face in his hands, concern in his eyes. 'Samia, I can't live without you. It's that simple. The power of what I feel for you overwhelms me. I thought it was just passion—physical passion—and I'd seen what that did to my father. I thought I was displaying all of his crazy possessive and destructive traits. But the difference was that he never loved my mother. And love is the difference.'

If was as if there was some final brick in the wall that was guarding her heart—which was pathetic because Sadiq already had the power to crush her to pieces if he so wished. But something was holding her back from letting go. Perhaps it was her own fear of love, after seeing how it had destroyed those closest to her.

Sadiq could see it in her face, and suddenly he took her hand and tugged her after him. 'I'll show you something. Maybe then you'll believe.'

Samia wiped at her wet cheeks, almost stumbling after

Sadiq because he was walking so fast. He stopped outside a door that was on the same corridor, and took a deep breath before opening it.

It was a beautiful room, with blue and green wallpaper and sumptuous divans piled high with cushions. A window opened out onto a small private terrace and B'harani glittered in the distance. But the thing that Samia noticed most was in the centre of the room, in pride of place.

She let go of Sadiq's hand. She could feel his tension as she walked towards the piano, running her hand reverently over the bittersweetly familiar lines. With silent tears running down her face she turned back to Sadiq. 'My mother's piano. You brought it here.'

He nodded. 'I arranged with your brother to have it sent here the night after you told me what had happened to you.' He looked disarmingly unsure of himself. 'I wanted to do something... But if you don't want it...'

Samia shook her head, and the last piece of the wall fell apart. She walked back to Sadiq and stretched up to take his face in her hands to kiss him. She felt his relief, and exulted in the brief moment of insecurity he'd shown.

When she could stop kissing him she pulled back and said, 'How long has it been here?'

Sadiq smiled ruefully. 'About two weeks. But every time I thought I'd tell you I came up with an excuse, because I knew damn well that the minute you saw it you'd know exactly how I felt...'

Samia kissed him again, her heart singing. 'You're an idiot, but I love you.'

Sadiq started to pull her from the room and Samia looked back at the piano wistfully. Sadiq said fondly, 'You can come back. But I want to take you to one more place.'

Samia was floating on a cloud of bliss. She would have gone anywhere on the earth with Sadiq, and she followed him obediently to his Jeep, then a helicopter. Her heart started to pound when she saw the familiar lines of the castle at Nazirat. But they were flying over the castle, and when Samia saw where they were landing something dark pierced her haze of happiness.

If there was one place on the earth she could have avoided, it would have been the bedouin tent.

Sadiq picked up on her tension and took her hand as they got out of the helicopter. He took her face in his hands once it had lifted away into the skies again, leaving them utterly alone.

'Just trust me, okay?'

Samia nodded and bit her lip. It was almost excruciating to remember that night, and the thought that he'd been here with all those other women.

The sun was setting and painting everything a gorgeous burnished gold as she followed Sadiq into the tent again. She gasped with shock when she saw that it had been completely redecorated. Nothing remained from that night.

He pulled her around in front of him and said carefully, 'Samia, I've never brought any other woman here. Only you. This tent didn't exist until I had it built for us when we were in the castle. But that night…' He shook his head in disgust at himself. 'I think that was the start of it. I'd brought you here and suddenly you were questioning me. I couldn't believe how transparent I'd been.'

Joy was infusing every cell of Samia's body. She smiled. 'I thought I had to let you know straight away that I wasn't seeing it as a romantic gesture, but all I wanted was to believe that you'd done this for *me*.'

Sadiq pulled her close, where she could feel how badly he wanted her, and the last few nights of sleeplessness and aching and wanting rose up within Samia like a forest fire. Much like the last time, but in completely different circumstances, they were on the bed, making love with an intensity that made Samia cry out over and over again.

Much later, when their bodies were just a tangle of limbs, dark against pale, Sadiq was trailing Samia's hair through his hand and he said quietly, 'Now I know why I was so freaked out when I saw Nadim and Salman get married.'

Samia lifted her heavy head and came up on one elbow to look at her husband. 'What do you mean?'

Sadiq brushed her hair back over her shoulder, and the tender look on his face and in his eyes made Samia feel extraordinarily blessed. She caught his injured hand and kissed it.

'Because I knew that I was terrified of being as emotionally exposed as they were in those moments. And then you came along, and any hope of protecting myself from a similar fate flew out the window.'

Samia grumbled good-naturedly, 'You took long enough to come around to the idea...'

Sadiq flipped up to hover over her, covering her sensitised breasts with his chest, making her squirm against him deliciously. He smiled. 'And I'm going to spend our lifetimes paying you back for taking so long to recognise what was in my own heart. It'll be a long and slow and infinite process...'

Samia wound her arms around his neck and arched even closer, exulting in his rapidly recovering arousal. 'I like the sound of long and slow, Sultan...so what are you waiting for?'

* * * * *

SEPTEMBER 2011 HARDBACK TITLES

ROMANCE

The Kanellis Scandal	Michelle Reid
Monarch of the Sands	Sharon Kendrick
One Night in the Orient	Robyn Donald
His Poor Little Rich Girl	Melanie Milburne
The Sultan's Choice	Abby Green
The Return of the Stranger	Kate Walker
Girl in the Bedouin Tent	Annie West
Once Touched, Never Forgotten	Natasha Tate
Nice Girls Finish Last	Natalie Anderson
The Italian Next Door...	Anna Cleary
From Daredevil to Devoted Daddy	Barbara McMahon
Little Cowgirl Needs a Mum	Patricia Thayer
To Wed a Rancher	Myrna Mackenzie
Once Upon a Time in Tarrula	Jennie Adams
The Secret Princess	Jessica Hart
Blind Date Rivals	Nina Harrington
Cort Mason – Dr Delectable	Carol Marinelli
Survival Guide to Dating Your Boss	Fiona McArthur

HISTORICAL

The Lady Gambles	Carole Mortimer
Lady Rosabella's Ruse	Ann Lethbridge
The Viscount's Scandalous Return	Anne Ashley
The Viking's Touch	Joanna Fulford

MEDICAL ROMANCE™

Return of the Maverick	Sue MacKay
It Started with a Pregnancy	Scarlet Wilson
Italian Doctor, No Strings Attached	Kate Hardy
Miracle Times Two	Josie Metcalfe

**SEPTEMBER 2011
LARGE PRINT TITLES**

ROMANCE

Too Proud to be Bought	Sharon Kendrick
A Dark Sicilian Secret	Jane Porter
Prince of Scandal	Annie West
The Beautiful Widow	Helen Brooks
Rancher's Twins: Mum Needed	Barbara Hannay
The Baby Project	Susan Meier
Second Chance Baby	Susan Meier
Her Moment in the Spotlight	Nina Harrington

HISTORICAL

More Than a Mistress	Ann Lethbridge
The Return of Lord Conistone	Lucy Ashford
Sir Ashley's Mettlesome Match	Mary Nichols
The Conqueror's Lady	Terri Brisbin

MEDICAL ROMANCE™

Summer Seaside Wedding	Abigail Gordon
Reunited: A Miracle Marriage	Judy Campbell
The Man with the Locked Away Heart	Melanie Milburne
Socialite...or Nurse in a Million?	Molly Evans
St Piran's: The Brooding Heart Surgeon	Alison Roberts
Playboy Doctor to Doting Dad	Sue MacKay

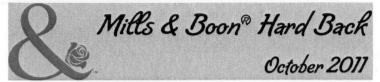

Mills & Boon® Hard Back

October 2011

ROMANCE

The Most Coveted Prize	Penny Jordan
The Costarella Conquest	Emma Darcy
The Night that Changed Everything	Anne McAllister
Craving the Forbidden	India Grey
The Lost Wife	Maggie Cox
Heiress Behind the Headlines	Caitlin Crews
Weight of the Crown	Christina Hollis
Innocent in the Ivory Tower	Lucy Ellis
Flirting With Intent	Kelly Hunter
A Moment on the Lips	Kate Hardy
Her Italian Soldier	Rebecca Winters
The Lonesome Rancher	Patricia Thayer
Nikki and the Lone Wolf	Marion Lennox
Mardie and the City Surgeon	Marion Lennox
Bridesmaid Says, 'I Do!'	Barbara Hannay
The Princess Test	Shirley Jump
Breaking Her No-Dates Rule	Emily Forbes
Waking Up With Dr Off-Limits	Amy Andrews

HISTORICAL

The Lady Forfeits	Carole Mortimer
Valiant Soldier, Beautiful Enemy	Diane Gaston
Winning the War Hero's Heart	Mary Nichols
Hostage Bride	Anne Herries

MEDICAL ROMANCE™

Tempted by Dr Daisy	Caroline Anderson
The Fiancée He Can't Forget	Caroline Anderson
A Cotswold Christmas Bride	Joanna Neil
All She Wants For Christmas	Annie Claydon

Mills & Boon® Large Print

October 2011

ROMANCE

Passion and the Prince	Penny Jordan
For Duty's Sake	Lucy Monroe
Alessandro's Prize	Helen Bianchin
Mr and Mischief	Kate Hewitt
Her Desert Prince	Rebecca Winters
The Boss's Surprise Son	Teresa Carpenter
Ordinary Girl in a Tiara	Jessica Hart
Tempted by Trouble	Liz Fielding

HISTORICAL

Secret Life of a Scandalous Debutante	Bronwyn Scott
One Illicit Night	Sophia James
The Governess and the Sheikh	Marguerite Kaye
Pirate's Daughter, Rebel Wife	June Francis

MEDICAL ROMANCE™

Taming Dr Tempest	Meredith Webber
The Doctor and the Debutante	Anne Fraser
The Honourable Maverick	Alison Roberts
The Unsung Hero	Alison Roberts
St Piran's: The Fireman and Nurse Loveday	Kate Hardy
From Brooding Boss to Adoring Dad	Dianne Drake